Duggan

Montayj

Original publication date: February 14, 2013
Republication date: June 19, 2015

Duggan (republished)

Published by Jones House Publishing
Copyright 2015 by Jones House Publishing

ISBN-13: 978-0692476406
ISBN-10: 0692476407

Stories in this novel are merely a fictional recreation of events that may or may have not occurred. All characters bearing similarity to real life characters are made-up and not based on anyone in particular.

Jones House Publishing
joneshousepublishing@gmail.com
www.joneshousepublishing.com

Dedicated to the old spirits of Duggan whose spirits still travel the thoroughfares and keep watch over the bodies of the neighborhood like the ancestors.

Special thanks to anyone who has ever stepped foot in The Park and touched my life, whether knowingly or unknowingly.

Jones House Publishing

"If Duggan ever dies as a neighborhood, then we will die as a society." ~~ Anonymous

Section One:

Introduction

Only If Hope Was Real

In the beginning, before summer nights became especially long, boring occasions with unwilling participants, there had been an excitement about life that filled the air, making it thick with laughter. Brothers and sisters, aunts and uncles, nieces and nephews, new and old friends, once in a while strangers all gathered around back porches narrating past tales of pleasure once given to them by their elders while the youngest children played games out in the yard: the hop scotches, the hide-n-go-seeks, the red-light-green-lights, and occasionally, the yard fights between cousins that lasted for hours, off again on again, because the grownups were often too drunk to care or perhaps wanted the kids to learn a lesson on their own doing. Most mornings, the sweet smell of cooling buttermilk biscuits from grandmama's oven made the kids forget about their disagreement and worked wonders in curing hangovers for the adults; on Sundays, the aroma of pine needle tea, which was always grandmama's favorite, pervaded every corner of the house. Those were the days that seemed given to them by God. Everyone in the family, the old, the young, the wannabe adults, and the middle-aged adults treasured Sundays because it gave them a chance to kick back and forget about the hard work from the week before that was about to begin again.

It was in the beginning that little flowers that look like Texas bluebonnets bloomed alongside wild morning-glories. Baby robins crooned in their nests while their mothers were out gathering a breakfast of worm, fallen bread crumb, or whatever items that had been tossed carelessly to the ground. Moss grew alongside knarred trees and yellowish-white mushrooms burgeoned without marring the evenly planted grass.

Gerald and Jackie anticipated, very quietly, the arrival of their third child. For him, it was his second, both by her, and for her, her fourth, one of which, whose name was Hope, was no longer living.

Unheated summer nights, which are very rare in particular southern areas, sported the very air that they breathed. They watched, with starry, anticipative eyes as love shed itself of its time-dependent barrier, like a cocoon torn away from its silk inner covering.

The occasion had been one of beauty.

From time to time, attributable to the inconsistency in love, the days that they shared were tended by all of the fortunes in life and none of its misfortunes.

It was a fairytale beginning that even the books could not script.

*

Soon, the happiness they experienced as young lovers vanished and was replaced by depressionary times. The second summer of their being together kicked in like snares, opening the doors to seventeen weeks of impetuous warmth. Temperature flirted around ninety-five degrees for about a month, disguised as a passionate holocaust; and the humidity was a suppressing blanket of heat. Day in, day out, heat waves vanquished the atmosphere as suffocating quilts of fire erupted from sunrays like active volcanic lava spills.

And yet, as the atmospheric crisis played its toll on Gerald, just being together was enough to keep Jackie content. But what of love could there be to hold together the links in a chain and prevent corrosion when the availability of financial oil is so little? Still, Jackie rejoiced to Gerald's dissatisfaction. While the wife throve off a love that only a woman could feel, pressure ripped away the spinal cord of his sanity savagely, leaving him feeling powerless, hollow, blank. And he suffered from lack; for instance, money was shorn, or, in fact, cut off from their particular household. Bills poured in like rain showers, submerging the two of them under the ocean's floor. Insufficiently, they scratched and scraped and borrowed but were penniless. Children cried out from a shortage of food.

"Mama, we hungry," through snot-filled noses.

When the house stood stationary one could hear their stomachs growling as if their insides were eating itself, silently roaring as vomit was being constructed by fragments of bread and contaminated water; and without any health insurance and increasing bills, the children suffered from sundry, uncured illnesses.

"Gerald, because we got married you know they denied my Medicaid. State said they won't pay for it as long as they know there's a man in the house. The kids need it. What if one was to get sick? And I'm not talking about just a common cold. I mean really sick, or broke a leg, or something worse. I don't care if I don't have it, but the kids, they're so helpless."

"We can't afford it," and he turned his attention to the football game.

Jackie's plea, having been denied, did not lose existence. She just tucked it away for a better time.

One night while the family was asleep, Jessica, Jackie's second child, snuck into the kitchen for a late night snack only to find the kitchen stripped of its provisions. Dirty dishes bonded together as they made refuge in the sink. Trash piles gathered up in every corner. In the middle of the floor lay oil-stained rags, dirty diapers, and soured toothbrushes. With every footstep she took, the floor squeaked, and one soft part poorly built acted as a sponge to diversity and nearly collapsed as small footsteps trampled across it. The light from the kitchen was dim as dripping water from the sink produced a melodramatic rhythm that is only heard in decaying ghetto homes. She opened the refrigerator door with the hopes of revealing food but emptiness prevailed. The only available sources were that of baking soda, a box of corn flakes, water, butter, and an old bag of potato chips.

"I wish we was rich," Jessica sighed, staring gravely at the unfilled refrigerator. "I wish we was rich."

Roaches paraded around the inside of the refrigerator territorially. Jessica pushed them aside, unmoved by their touch, to show them that she was much more powerful than they were, but mostly out of hunger.

"Move," she whispered, really out of despair because she had learned to blank out their disgusting presence.

Three o'clock in the morning Jackie was awakened from her sleep by the hot sweat that stirred on her back, leaving her side of the bed saturated and sour. Without rousing her snoring husband, she sneaked out of bed into a less oppressive part of the house. As she fingered her way through the dark, an unbalanced, crunching sound greatly disturbed her. Flicking on the light switch she found her daughter sitting on the couch eating corn flakes and water.

"Oh baby," faded with the crunching sound.

*

Fundamentally, how could Jackie even begin to assume that she had recovered from her idealized nightmare that had begun when she had that car wreck some time earlier that took the life of her daughter? Gerald had come and carried her off to fairyland; Jessica brought her back…

*

It was now August, the hottest month of the year in Texas, and the sun disguised itself perfectly in the sky, masquerading behind big, fluffy, white clouds. And at the right time no one would have even known that it was there had it not been for the skin tanning steam that was reflected from the paved streets that absorbed it. Wind blew at every chance it could seize an opportunity, collecting dust from ditches and gutters and interlacing it with the other sordid particles floating aimlessly into the southern winds; and this wind was incredibly hot, making the street hustlers yearn for changing weather. And their wishes were granted with a melancholic rain.

At home, Jackie sat rocking in a chair full of hurt, staring into a blank gulf. Head nearly empty of feeling. Nothing was there to fill the void in her mind. Stomach knotting. She had come home two days earlier and found Jessica shaking on the floor. It was Hope all over again! Jackie's heart joggled, and clear, purified liquids fell slowly from her heart and into her stomach. It was a powerful descent, such is the unseen cascades of anguish. She did not touch her daughter's vibratile body, but kind of fell back into a corner, rocking as if she held her daughter in her arms, too afraid to upset the fragile heap twisting on the floor.

"Come back to me, Jessica! Come back to me. I'm right here. Do you hear me, child. Come back to me! Don't do this to me. Not now, Jessy. Not now. Come back to mama."

Not only had Jessica made her mother's heart cry but she had gone and got herself sick. It resulted in more pain, more loneliness, stripping the family of one more of its members, not to the death, but to a state controlled facility.

Nightfall had just vanquished the daylight. Outside it rained harder than before. Jackie tried to recall the last time that it rained this hard but her memory was inexact. Gumball-sized drops of rain beat loudly against the antiquated house and nearly lacerated the windows. From each direction rain swarmed down roughly, drowning out any other sounds of the world. The world pleasantly shed its tears without much accompaniment from other weather-related aspects for a while.

As Mother Nature ruled the outside, the inside of the house was controlled by Gerald. When he talked, he roared like Mother Nature was in his throat, words rolling from his tongue like a tempest, most of which were filtered. Jackie only made out the most damaging ones.

"Lazy." "Whore." "Nothing ass, neglectful bitch." "Unfit." "Never should've married a piece of shit." "Hate your ass."

Wind scratched terribly at the roof. The rain, a steady downfall. Tree limbs rose and descended in one apparent motion. Bead-like lightning ripped the sky into segments. A streak of blood marred Jackie's face... from the thunder... from the rain...a projecting fist... gushing wind... the painful declaration of: "Stop...Not in front of my children..."

But what is a plea for help in a remote wood but the unheard noise of a fallen tree? Those kinds of creativities are sucked up by all that green life and never make it to civilization. Simply, help becomes: "Go to hell..."

For each blow that he delivered to her tiny face in an attempt to actually beat her down into hell, she uttered a nasty, elongated shrill for help responding to the pain but the rain made her cries seem like whispers. Her children screamed too but even they could not hear their own cries—sounds that were buried beneath the thumping of rain against the shabby old house frame. Each cry devitalized like fading ink. For twenty-two minutes Gerald attacked her violently, uncontrollably. He had promised her that he would never hurt her... That hurting her would cause his living death, and he would rather be lost in space before he laid hands upon such beauty... When he tired out he left her battered, tearless even, and squawking in the dirt that resided on the floor. Out the door he went, disappearing into the flourishing rain. That was the end of their eight year marriage.

*

Loneliness was all that Jackie knew. Vines of it

grew around her heart like armor protecting the dear life of some poor warriors. Loneliness was dark. When her hands fumbled for a light switch, her fingers seemed to vanish into thin air.

*

...She no longer followed the movement of time. She woke up one morning to an empty bed and knew that she no longer had her husband or daughter...

*

Eight weeks of inactivity turned Jackie's financial independence into a more lowly state. She was now living in a small, wooded in apartment complex ran by an intense breathing, corpulent white man. The apartment's secondary name had been Wilshire Apartments when the ruling class of Montgomery County were going around tagging the lame, communal buildings with upper-class names, trying to gentrify—by title only—the back end of Duggan. The tenants who rented these apartments knew them for what they were: 'The Bricks,' and the landlord, one Jonah Bush, seemed fitting for renting out these apartments. Dilapidation spilled over the entire region like acid rain, deteriorating both the courtyard and the flats that people called home. But they were cheap so Jackie was satisfied.

*

It never appeared as if Jackie's sadness would end. It just seemed like it had infinities protecting it. Queer vines kept growing and growing. She never thought plant life could be so plentiful in such arctic temperature that was taking over her seasons.

*

The winter rolled around like a smothering blanket of glacial rime. Jackie sat 'Indian-style' in a corner warming herself by an electrical heater, gazing at her children who, one by one, produced a face painting of hunger and exhaustion. Outside, hail descended lightly, knocking against rusting tin-plated rooftops, scratching gently at windowpanes, and overlying the streets with flattened chunks of ice. Roads were slippery and wet. Ice hugged onto trees giving their barks a glistening moist texture. The life of humans was nearly nonexistent save for a few junkies and prostitutes of all colors standing on street corners. Potholes that plagued the entrance into the gated apartments were cemented solid with hardened water. Ditches and gutters were altered to fit the outlook of bayous of flimsy ice skating ponds.

Jackie gazed through the window, through clefts of descending ice, wondering how long it would last, this unexpected, heatless winter filled with the whiteness of an undeviating, rich season, but for her a nuclear winter.

"I wonder how long it's gone be like this?" she said mostly to herself than to her kids.

By now she was beside herself with depression: a circulation of grief overwhelmed her completely; shattered hopes and dreams; a misplaced husband; a pocketbook only worth the price of a peso; a withering body frame, which she now saw as she stared at herself in a cracked mirror that hung loosely on the wall, clinging for dear life. Out of dismay, she snatched the mirror from its supportive peg and watched it shatter into a thousand tiny pieces. Just like her family life growing up. Just like her marriage. Just like her dead baby Hope. Just like her connection with Jessica. Just like her desired happy life.

*

Cold weather was not meant to bear only mortality. If it loses existence, it dies and reincarnates into something greater than before…

*

Soft, frozen water touched her face as she ambled up and down the dimly lit, deserted street, fighting her way through strong recurring winds that cuffed against her shivering, frosted skin. Under a grey sky she walked, teeth chattering with a soft reverberation as cold weather began to dominate her failing body heat. Nothingness all around. Accompanied by a dropping temperature. A fog crawling backwards. It moved like the unseen navy of loneliness, westward, northward, leaving behind a trail of confusion. Yet and still, the sights of the world remained the same with its continuance of a one-sided color distribution: whiteness jumping out to meet her eyes. Up and down. In angles. Eastward, southward. And it all seemed as if it were a part of a dream... for the aspect of dreams—which dawned in the snow—was all around. And it was that beautiful dream aspect that opened encased memories in her mind. Recollections of nostalgia. Coming, but seemingly, never going. Mentally destroying her as she regressed to the early years where memories and pain were all that she had. The pain of memories mounting, and the more she thought about it the more the memories became unshakable, the more concrete became the pain, the more her remembrances made her want to be rid of her cursed and hopeless life.

She said to herself: "Not now. I don't want to remember," but it was too late.

She could not keep her mind from drifting to those heartrending, early childhood experiences that were just like the present night in some regards: still one-colored with a retrogressing snow fog and an angry wind or with emptiness clinging to her spirit. Then her thirteen year old self would be born again, conjuring up even the most elusive elements of her dreams. But it was the realness, the solidity of dreams that held the substance that made her feel what no one else but her could feel—a faraway pain aided by faraway memories:

It was cold. Sun barely shining. Wind at a standstill because by then snow no longer fell but sat idly on the ground waiting to melt, to be sucked back into the clouds by evaporation only to repeat its descent, this time, maybe, as a rain. Six gentlemen callers. One house. One room. One female. One opening between the legs. Soreness. Monotonous stroking. Exaggerated screams. Time and time again. Then came the hatred for her mother. The hate that grew with the years.

Jackie whispering, "Mama, don't make me hate you."

The hate that she protected. The mortification. The bitterness. The blistering resentment. And the vow to be nothing like her mother when she grew up.

"I promise mama, I will not become you," as she looked in the bedroom mirror at her young self.

But she was, in so many ways. And oh! how her

every dream was interlaced with the sadness. Jackie's sadness. And she alone had to bear that sadness.

Beautiful Jackie Pickens stood on Crooke Street gazing into the lingering darkness—inwardly, cheered by faith, but outwardly, at a loss of hope—searching for life. But just like most nights before the streets were deficient. Not a creeping shadow to fill the void of stray darkness that outlined the gentle night.

The snow fell singularly to the ground in a steady pulse, beating the ground like leaking faucet water. But softer. And the softer it fell the louder it became. Jackie listened to the sound of fallen snow by pressing her ear to the wind... euphonious, like a soft, mellow combination of words—a pleasant resonance—written in Braille... until it stopped, and the sky began to clear. Soon, the sun would come and dissect the night and Jackie would be left, once again, to stand and wonder...

She wrapped her arms around her body for warmth. The cold pain that she experienced dampened her spirits. She no longer cared for the existence of the snow, or for standing like a dummy in the cold, downcast, nor for the existence of her optimistic mind. She felt as if she was being shed of the romantic things that misleadingly surrounded her life until they no longer survived. Without it, all she had were those things of existence: the no longer falling snow; the crestfallen feelings;   and the painful nostalgic memories.

There had been dreary nights before; nights that packed up and carried away joy; nights where the cold weather would reemphasize her crucial position; nights where she felt like giving up; but none like this.

"I don't deserve this!" she shouted to no one in particular. "I don't deserve this!" to the sky. "I really don't!" to the pavement. Then softly and unsurely to herself: "I just don't."

Just as she was about to walk home Jackie shifted her body in time to notice a white car creeping without the accompaniment of light. The car pulled up just a few feet in front of her. Jackie stepped back to widen the distance. There was a strange burning smell coming from the front of the car that had been weakened as a result of the cold air. The window squeaked when it rolled down, like it hadn't been used in a long time. Jackie cringed at the sound. It reminded her of Jessica, how she used to climb out of the bedroom window, the way the window would squeak at the very moment Jessica thought she was being slick. Jackie laughed, but it was only a suppressed chortle. In the dark her eyes looked like little Christmas ornaments for the cold had settled and left glistening moisture on her brows. However dark or not, her beauty could not be denied.

She heard a rough grumble that broke through her protective barrier that sounded sort of like: - "Get in," formed out of the vortex of a nasty, suppressed cough.

Stillness, as if a wicked spark from a shooting star, spread itself over the night, while those two words continued to erode… and the confusion that was eventually caused by the cold, which made the words lose significance, made Jackie out to be a stiff mass of frozen flesh…

… until, "Get in," was cautiously repeated…

…and Jackie climbed in upon his second appeal, uneasy, unsure…

They drove around the west parts of Duggan repeatedly, making a noose around one block: Crooke Street, Avenue I, Park Place, Avenue K. From there they drove to Kasmiersky Park in the Westwood part of Pals where Jackie seemed but an inadequate thought wafting within a larger, more profound conscious.

-'Edgy there gal?'

-'Huh?'

-'Don't be.'

-'Be what?'

-'Relax.'

-'I am relaxed.'

-'Then why are you shaking?'

-'I'm a little cold,' Jackie said.

-'But it's not cold in the car.'

-'Sure, whatever.'

She bit her lips as they trembled from heat warming her body. He saw how often she shivered when he spoke; therefore, not to scare away his little trapped deer, he kept his sentences short and clear.

-'Are you scared?'

-'No.'

Her lies were as transparent as her fear. He smelt it. They drove along in silence, her staring into the night, he into her beautiful Black face for several seconds before continuing the tense conversation.

-'How much?'

-'What?'

-'How much?' He tilted his head forward just enough to show sarcasm but not for her to make out his face. 'For what we are about to engage in?'

-'Oh.' Recapturing the confusion. 'Two-hundred dollars.'

-'Huh gal, damn?'

-She replied, 'Two-hundred,' this time with more coolness.

-'Shit gal, you sure are high.'

-'That's my price, man; your ass ain't came to Duggan this late at night without your pocketbook I know?' She paused and touched her chin. 'I can get out if that pleases you. I'm not one of those twenty dollar hookers man. This here is a diamond.'

Jackie said this to hide the fear she felt by being near him and of losing a customer more than anything. Her high price meant she would be worth every cent. He pondered over the proposal for a second and managed to squeeze out an 'Okay,' as if he were the one in submission and drove off.

By the time he stopped the car they were parking deep by the woods where there was no form of life moving about, only the growing hands of colorlessness. Stars reached out and snatched their scintillation away from the night as if in quarrel with the dark. The quasars and night, intimate connection, like the mind and temporary insanity, it all walked away from the light with laughter tucked inside of its brassiere...

Time came when the gentleness that this strange man once displayed vanished, quickly turning into hunger, lust. Sitting next to him after an overextended period caused Jackie to shudder. It was the nearness that underlined her terror and concern although they were not yet fully realized emotions. It was the nearness that drew her closer and closer to him while subconsciously holding her distant. The nearness of his hands. The nearness of his face. His crooked smile. And that salesman-pitched voice. The familiarity of it all. Even the laid back chuckle. So pure that it became unrecognizable. The inflections made by the conscious—like the inner strings of the mind were being plucked—kept crying out to him in strange, rhythmic intonations, noises that were unclear to Jackie, like two kids skipping under the shining sun on a rainy day, unable to hear their mother's dinner call; the rest, blurred by the present environment. Sudden, internal noises that he was unsure if he should listen to; conscious speaking as if in a trance of abandoned words. The divide that held him was strong and he painfully struggled against his will and his desire.

Darkness has a way of controlling a person's soul, making them do and say things that are not a part of who they are. "I am enchanted by your long and silky Black hair."

He touched it. Jackie felt his fingers fumbling each strand. It kind of disgusted her. He shot her an intense gaze that went far beyond her eyes. He told her how beautiful they were; Jackie only sighed. Till now she hadn't really cared to look at him to notice anything about him as closely as he examined her. He was only a white blob that she could make disappear.

"Your lips are like something of the arts."

He touched them with the back of his index finger, the upper, then the lower. She shuddered, noticeably.

"You are a strange one," Jackie muttered beneath her breath, half hoping that he didn't hear and partly hoping that he did.

His blue eyes sunk deep into his colorless face, and both became blurred invisibilities, like stars sucked into the Milky Way. He grabbed her by the face as if he were going to lay a big wet kiss upon her lips, but his grip was far too tight for the kissing. Without ever having experienced it, Jackie knew what this grip symbolized, knew its pains, its eternal memories. When she was young she used to have dreams about it and she would sit in the corner of her room and shake until the horror passed. As she grew older, the dreams disappeared but became untouchable images that she could hardly see—fuzzy reflections. She knew what they were, why they were there, and why they were no longer in dream form. Instead of sitting in her bedroom corner she sat in the kitchen corner, on the side of the refrigerator, and rocked, always trying to touch the image, to tear that opaque figure away from her mother and the entire image from her mind.

When Jackie was young she used to dream about all of the things that she would do and be when she grew into a young lady. She would sit in her grandmother's lap and read about princesses and all of the nice things they had, the emeralds, the rubies, the pearls, the castle, and of the innocent-eyed princes and knights who guarded against evil dragons. She held onto this dream for as long as she could, daring to see it slip away. His words were callous when they came again, but had a hint of spinelessness to them, just like the smoky figure in her images: 'List-en... you... colored... wench... scream... and I will break... your... fu-ckin'... neck...'

He spoke slowly and clearly, struggling with his words purposely so that she would understand each syllable, almost as if every word he spoke was hyphenated.

Paralysis, as a result of fear, can sometimes be impossible to overcome. Jackie sat in the car stiff, like the dead hands of a clock unyielding to the movement of time, barely breathing, heart barely beating, eyes barely flinching, continuously staring. The only true motion sited on her was the invisible downpour of tears rolling down both cheeks where water would have been had she been able to express her grief, with or without sound. A lump rooted in her throat when she tried to speak, causing her to mum her cry for help. Empty words escaped her mouth. She was trying to scream, to let the world around know, to let herself know, that she was still alive. She closed her eyes and imagined that she was at home, in bed, with her children, safe, and not under the entrancing influences of dehumanization.

A small conundrum drifted: the stereotypical aspects of man—the dominant force over woman, and the dark, dominance over life—and Jackie found herself thinking, wishing, that he would just die, and that right fast. The clarity of the impending danger had finally reached her.

Naturally, she could not stop it from occurring: thick, yellow fingernails digging deep into both of her cheeks; flashing brown teeth tearing at the nipples on her breasts. From her perforated skin, blood ran in staggered streaks like bead lightning and she did not grasp onto the fact that she was bleeding until the hot liquid began to burn her flesh. The strange man looked at her in the eyes and Jackie could see in his red, reptilian eyes the radiation coming from them. The dark red crave glowing in his smile. What had once been her sacred and protected garden was about to be picked clean of all its fruitfulness.

He seized her, stretched out across her body as

much as room would allow, smothering her body with his obese white flesh. He had infiltrated her palace and there was no protection against that, no biased judges to decide right from wrong, just he and her. It was all so unreal to the queen who lay in a dream-like state, staring at the sex-driven monster on top of her.

Gerald Thompson was her husband. He was good to her. Gave her two children. Loved the other two she had out of wedlock, even the dead one—Hope—whose heart just stopped beating. Said fuck to her past. All he cared about was her. Him. Now. She was all he needed. Her heart beat regularly during those days. Pulsed like the sun handing out its rays on an early June morning. He promised her that he would make her happy. He tried but they were extremely poor. It hurt him. Made him feel like the inferior being that he so feared. He was blind and impatient. Even though he could not see it, she was very happy. Even more satisfied. He was all she ever wanted. They could have made it and she knew it. But poverty pulled them apart. She was alone. Gerald Thompson was her husband.

Her eyes tightened, constricted and slanted, and her legs defied all rules of flexibility, pulling back like a slingshot, stretching without tearing, and she came to the point of release, like two sharp-edged rocks projecting, but it was the elbows and head that became connected, and it was he who felt the inadequacies of pain, as he fell backward out of her mythical sky.

"Damn bitch," he cried more than he yelled.

Gerald Thompson carried her off into enchantment. He was good to her until he beat her. She was all he ever wanted. He loved her but he left her.

Jackie had the passenger door open, attempting to escape when he grabbed her and they went tumbling onto the hardened ground—she nearly in her birthday suit, and he with a torn shirt and breeches pulled down about his ankles—directly upon pinecones, sticks, and sharp rocks that dug into her back.

"You ain't goin' nowhere," he breathed.

They struggled under an invisible wintry sky, Jackie for emancipation, he for restraint.

"Get off me," she struggled. "Let me loose!"

Eventually, she climbed to her feet and ran with unnoticeable speed but as she reached the south end of the park a hole in the ground snagged her right foot from under her, stopping her forcefully in her tracks; and from the speed in which she ran the impact completely shattered her ankle. She let out a terrifying cry and fell to the ground, trapped in her own misery. True self-misery. And it was incredibly real how nameless pain claimed her body wholly and as she checked on her foot she could see white bone sticking out of her skin. She nearly fainted.

"Awww!" she sighed loudly.

The repulsive sight suffocated her cries and she lie on the ground, face full of tears, grass, and dirt, mute.

During the brief intermission the strange man had climbed back inside his car and grabbed a rusty switch blade and now stood over her, sneering at her with spittle dripping from his red mouth like big rain droplets. *Mama, if a man ever rapes you I will kill him for you, I promise...* Heavy grunts disturbed her and brought her back from reminiscence.

All Jackie could utter was, 'My leg. My leg.'

Her pleas were muffled out when the man stepped on her stomach wickedly with a frosty-bitter, contaminated, pinkish foot, snapping blood and oxygen from her mouth.

'I hate your type. Think you're too good for old people like me.' He laughed, choking on blood that was interfused with his words. He stabbed her gently with quick punches, not really penetrating the skin.

Jackie bellowed some strange words but they

were feeble coming from the mouth and slightly hindered by trickling blood.

"Please stop," was slightly heard.

Dim light from the basketball court dawned above them like the fading sun drowning in the far horizon. And it all came together, interwoven naturally like the colors of a rainbow: the balding and rotund wrinkled scalp; the wide body frame that overwhelmed her smallness, enveloping her into an ocean of white shadow. The voice. Rape you then stab you. The laugh. And the massive teeth that she grew accustomed to from the evidence of the bite marks in her skin. But that wasn't it. There was something else. Something more unique. And it hit her when the strange man came close, putting his face right above hers in that faint light. It was her landlord Jonah!

He snarled something about her dying or about her meeting the one who created her; the words only hoped to penetrate the surface of her mind. She could not hear him. It was the pain. Mommy, why you always ignore me? You never hear a word that I ever say... But sometimes words do not transmit feeling... And yes, Gerald had cared for her enough to snatch the feeling right out of her heart... *Don't hit me... I'm sorry... Don't you believe me?... Don't you love me?... What did I do?... It won't happen again...* Forty-two times he stabbed her, never higher than the waist, but each perforation aimed towards the lower body area—thighs, legs, even once into her vagina—the rust-tipped knife like a ship that founders in the sea, gradually sinking into the ocean-like lump of brown flesh lying helplessly beneath him. *Mommy, what you doin'? Why that man layin' on top of you?* The daylight that was inside her began to wane but her body, shortly thereafter, still twitched. He shoveled the knife deep into her abdomen until the blade disappeared, seemingly ending her agony, her grief, because as her body sagged on the ground waiting to die, she looked helpless and defeated. She knew then that she had been abandoned by hope her entire life.

anatomy of black beauty

Her articulation is something that truly pacifies,
That gratifies me into a peace that easily solidifies.
She has a smile that recognizes and reconciles,
That negotiates peace through an aura that
amplifies;
Her walk—peacefully justifies,
It is a stroll where captivation abides;
Divinity in her smile,
celestial glints in her eyes,
and a nose that is beatified.

Aesthetic skin thou testify,
that of a love goddess; enchant me with love,
or leave my spirit mortified.
I despise only her lack of
Confidence that sometimes arise.
Searching for captivation of the spirit and why?
What makes her divine beyond time
Is a witty attitude that glorifies
A psychological imbalance of the mind.

Section Two

Ronny and Freddie:
Runaway Child

I

He left behind the unpretty things that shadowed him; hurt and the small amounts of pain that hovered inside; love because it depressed; and caring because it did not reciprocate. Left them behind like an unwanted thought in the subconscious; made them unthought so that they could no longer do harm; shut his eyes and imagined their nonexistence. The sadness would pass once he disconnected himself from their presence.

He sat at the back of the bus staring blankly at the falling rain, not really seeing the water but instead images of darkened, unemotional worlds that were reflected through the window. He longed to escape this world that he had been cast into, this Duggan world, but it seemed almost unshakable. But riding along on the inside of that bus he felt as if finally he would be able to begin to leave it behind. A teardrop fell slowly from his eye for the hope of possibly fleeing his hell.

Thunder reeled across the sky. Right then, the emptiness that had become his life was made vivid. Sounds and images roamed aimlessly through his mind, followed by fear, and he realized that even though the bus he rode was driving him away from Duggan, he would never be free of the memory, of his guilt. His day was dark like the innards of charcoal, and not just because of the rain, but more closely related to some strange feeling that he did not understand. He watched the small drops of water delicately tap the pane, seeing descended beads disperse into flattened drops before disappearing, like they were also running away.

His body trembled slightly like he had caught a chill. He wiped away a small amount of sweat that was trickling from his forehead with the back of his hand, then wrapped his arms around his body as if he were cold, though the bus itself was warm. A taste of old, stale blood lingered on his tongue and he was praying for his mind to be relieved of the images he was running from. He felt people's eyes burning through his skin although no one paid him any attention. He wanted to slip into a cave of solitude to escape reality, to live in a solitary state, even if it was only temporary. A small lump of despair migrated to his throat and made a home there for a while, making his mental anguish more complete. After what seemed like an eternity, his anxiety finally faded away.

Relaxing himself comfortably into his seat, an image of his mother invaded his thoughts. He could hear her yelling at him: "Get your black ass in there and clean up that damn room! And I mean now! After that, I want you to go out and find yourself a job. I got too many damn bills to be taken care of your grown ass!"

He smiled. His mother was such a pretty woman. She was medium-built, just over five feet, with short, stunning, kinky hair that was distinguished with gray strands of stress. Beautiful tan skin covered the small, sensuous features of her delicate body. Her thin eyes glittered from the ups and downs of life, and her smile anchored the love that she had for her children.

"What the hell have I done?" he kept mumbling to himself, eyes closed, head rocking, the bus moving along.

The rain came pouring down with great emotion, beating loudly against the thick windowpane. Lightning lit up the darkened sky into an unlasting daylight, followed by a loyal thunder. Another tear or two fell from his eyes as he gazed out of the wet window. In his twenty-two years of living he had never felt pain like the pain he was feeling now, he never knew loneliness like the loneliness he was experiencing now. His head fell back gently and unconstrained, agitating his neck, and out of weariness, he banged it softly against the window. Using his black bag as a pillow, he tried to fall asleep but it was impossible. He stared at the cream-white ceiling for about twenty-five minutes, lost in his own terrible thoughts.

II

Morning sunlight collided against the timeworn wall. Dirt particles floated in the streak of sunlight as if part of an ascending stairway, unsure whether to go up or down. A foul, heated odor invaded the ebbing living room and brought life to a daydreaming youth.

"What you gone do today?" Freddie asked with boredom aching in his voice. Ronny neither replied nor flinched; he just kept gazing at the clock with a fixed sensation. Freddie felt as if he'd been ignored, so he spoke with more intensity, slowly letting the words peel from his mouth. "Did you hear me man? I said what's up for the day?"

Nevertheless, Ronny remained silent. He just stared straight ahead, as if in a trance. Suddenly, he walked to the window like a mummy but did not look beyond the closed curtains.

"What's wrong wit' you man? You been trippin' all day and actin' real strange. I know you got somethin' on your mind 'cause this how you get when you up to somethin'. So let me know what the deal is?" Freddie asked once more, surveying Ronny's body language.

With a restrained undertaking, Ronny finally spoke up. "What you mean what I got up for the day? What do I do every single day that I'm above ground? Try to find a way to get money." He coughed out a snicker of despair directed more towards his personal musings rather than the natural objects of the world.

"So what do you wanna do today?" Freddie asked again, hoping for a straight answer.

"I don't know. Everyday it's the same ol' thang wit' us, you know. Wake up and try to avoid jail. Shower, brush our teeth, eat breakfast, watch TV till the sun go down, and then hustle. But the way the game is now, there is no real way for street pushers like us to make money. We fightin' a losin' battle right now. Wholesalers sellin' dopefiends the same thing they sellin us. The niggas we get the shit from don't wanna sell us nothin' half the time and then when they do we get shorted."

Freddie chimed in, "You ain't lyin' about that."

"Prices done went up in the streets but prices

ain't went up for the fiends and the fiends think we can sell them what the wholesalers sell 'em. We really gotta find a way to make a move, get out of street pushin'. We need to be wholesalin' by now too if we gone still be hustlin'."

"That's what I been sayin'," Freddie replied.

Ronny continued. "Them niggas are some hoes though on the cool. Think about it. Dudes that we grew up with, that we used to be cool with, they really look down us. They think they better than niggas like us just because they got a little money. Thang is, they ain't doin' shit with they money though. You feel me?"

Freddie nodded.

"They ain't buyin' no land. They ain't creatin' no jobs for niggas. They act like they rich but I bet they can't take two weeks off without feelin' the effects, just like we can't. We can get what they got by takin' what they got. Straight 'em up," Ronny continued.

He spoke with determination in his voice. His days of struggling in the brutal ghetto streets were beginning to take its affect. It felt as if he'd been shot in the neck by an unmoving bullet, one that had been dipped in lead-acid, that preyed on defenseless victims, leaving them weakened. The bullet, although fired only one time, multiplied and spread, producing a mass sufferance that he was now a part of. His pondering roused the depth of his childhood misery, and once again it was vivified. Standing on a pedestal there was pain, anguish, terror, images of his mother raising him single-handedly from birth and being a sole parent she could only do so much for him. The unknown, drunken father had run out on his mother while she was pregnant twenty-two years earlier not even knowing that the woman he slept with carried his unborn child. But Ronny didn't seem to care much about his fatherless childhood because he knew that his life was about to change drastically for he and his partner—one way or the other. He looked at Freddie and said, "I got a plan."

He walked into his bedroom without turning to see if Freddie would follow. He knew that he would because Freddie lived for excitement. What else did he have? He grew up in a broken home just as Ronny had and to bury his troubles he made his life an animation. In fact, the only thing that Freddie seemed afraid of was boredom.

Freddie jumped up from the sofa and stumbled into the bedroom like a little child on a Christmas morning racing to see what presents Santa, whom he knew to be his mother, had left the night before, only to find none. Once he entered Ronny locked his room door, separating them from any unwanted disturbances.

Freddie looked around in astonishment at a malformed room and thought to himself: *This is probably the only decent room in the whole house minus the filthy carpet that was plagued with dirt.* The only other room that he had the pleasure of exploring was the bathroom, a painted picture of despondency. Recurring on the ceiling as was on the floor was a mold, a dull, greenish-gray blemish. Preserved grittiness swamped the tub; the shower handle swung freely like a broken limb, and the commode, loosely connected to the floor, was old and no longer flushable. The door handle was missing and the door itself no longer shut with the perfection that it once had. The room reminded one of the Tulsa race riot devastation.

As he stared around in amazement, he thought sadly to himself how families in impoverished ghetto sectors always seem to be living in squalor and destitution. It hurt him to see his friend living like this, but what could he do? What could anyone do? He stared at Ronny, then at the discolored sheetrock on the ceiling, and murmured a little too loudly, "This is what poverty is like. This is truly the ghetto," to the quiet understanding of his friend.

One could only estimate the emotions being felt at that time. The only thing that was for sure was that they were there. They accumulated and scattered about, surrounding them with a pitch black nothingness. It wasn't anything new because they had been through it all their life, but for some reason this time seemed different.

Ronny sat down on the edge of the bed and examined the back of his hand for a brief minute. Freddie did the same like it was contagious. Then, in a silent whisper Ronny began to create, in stuttered words, a picture of climbing the social street ladder and leaving the old neighborhood. He had to get away, if not for anything else, just to be and feel born again, to have a childhood, to live! Yeah, it would be nice to experience that chance to see the joys of childhood living—even at twenty-two. He lived in what can be called a bottomless ocean and the water he swam in was deep, shark-infested, and his ship was always sinking.

Just listening to Ronny made it obvious that he couldn't take any more of the pain. It sounded as if one more occurrence of that *anymore* would strangulate his existence. Every uttered word dripped with old, struggling, never-had-no-hope blood. The time for change, or some kind of hope even, had long since passed and the only remaining opportunity foreseeable was taking matters into his own hands. For any ghetto child who has seen their opportunities turned into dust, is this not their only means of escapism from the cruelties of concrete life?

A fifteen second deadened hush exploded. Freddie looked at the floor as if the floor had been the one addressing him. A dumb expression engulfed his face and the lack of dexterity with his hands because of his inability to speak made it appear as if he were a mime trying to tear down the invisible wall that separated him from the light of understanding. "So when you wanna do this? And who you wanna get?" he shrieked after a late acknowledgment of Ronny's plan.

"We gettin' Green Eyes. I wanna do it tonight, if you down. I mean the sooner the better. All we got to do is get in and get out," Ronny said feeling the exuberance of his own suggestion touch him really for the first time as Freddie's excitement re-erected his nerves.

"Cool?" Freddie replied, greed gleaming in his sharp, rhombus-like eyes.

"I figure we go around 2:30, you know when all his boys is gone. Plus they don't really grind on Wednesdays since it be so slow. Gotta take a day off from hustlin' sometimes, huh? It won't be that hard. Fool thank he protected by his money."

The incredible thing about 2:30, Ronny thought, was that it symbolized a time of tranquility in the streets. The only time when peace could come out of its shelter. It was the time when dimness netted the street lights and the moon, no matter what quarter it was in, seemed to lose its life. Stillness prospered at 2:30 and the dark of night would always seem to reach its peak.

Their day's activities continued as usual until the evening's twilight decided to set in.

The late of night fell in slowly. Ronny and Freddie were growing anxious and it was evident by the way they paced around the small room.

"You wanna play some bones?" Ronny asked.

"Yeah, cool."

The decision that Ronny made to play dominos to pass the rest of the time was sating, and even though the time seemed to advance more slowly than before, this little game helped in alleviating their pain-stricken impatience. One hour later Ronny stared out of the window into a glaring light from a full moon, then looked at Freddie and said, "It's almost time, baby," more so with his eyes than his voice.

Within the next twenty minutes they were in Ronny's mother car, ready to go. Ronny wore his black Adidas, black Dickie suit, and a black beanie, disguising himself with the night, tossing Freddie a dark blue, similar outfit from his closet. He didn't intend to come back home with the same amount of cash that he had left with, a mere $137. His plan had to work.

The inside of the car was controlled by silence. At about 1:55 Ronny pulled away from the curb slowly and they were on their way. He was looking straight ahead. Only a visit from God himself could have broken his concentration. For the first time in his life he felt butterflies thickening in his stomach. They made his stomach bubble then tighten, repetitively. His grip strengthened around the steering wheel. The speed of the car immensely decreased as they began to drift towards a school zone.

Freddie settled himself comfortably in his seat, fastening his seatbelt to help control his jumpy body. He slid his gun under the seat, out of sight, grabbed a cigarette and lit it up. As he blew smoke out of his nose, he lowered the window slightly to feel the cool night air. The breeze was too cold for him so he let the window back up.

Ronny thought that this was a perfect night for jacking; the atmosphere was calm and the constant flow of breezes emerged to produce fair weather. The streets were scarce, not a single sole in sight. Mainly, there were no cops out patrolling, which greatly deleted their chances of being caught, so the scene was set. They rolled around the area about five or six times, then, Ronny pulled up on the dimly lit corner of Fifth Street and Avenue G, cut his lights, and parked his car at the end of the block; the rest of the task would be done on feet.

"This was it," Freddie thought aloud. "There ain't no turning back now."

It was all or nothing.

Ronny and Freddie clambered out of the car at the same time, cocking their guns back in a similar fashion, adding an unnecessary dramatic effect. They moved with caution toward the big brown house at the opposite end of the corner. Once they arrived they hopped over the fence instead of opening the gate, making as less noise as possible. They stole to the back and softly climbed the steps of the porch where more butterflies enhanced Ronny's nauseated stomach. With his gun in hand, Freddie kicked down the front door and they entered. A beautification stared at them that they weren't used to seeing in a home. The inside was spooky and they walked down a faint hallway holding on to the hand of regretfulness. In other words, it was something that had to be done due to their lack of money and they both knew and respected the consequences.

Just as expected, Green Eyes was sprawled out on the couch half drunk, half sleep. He was a large man with badly braided hair, and he wore a brand new three-piece pimp suit that fitted his wide body frame with imperfection. He acquired the nickname "Fatman," from some of the locals, not because of his size, but from his ruthless and wicked ways as a drug dealer. Greed had taken over Green Eyes' mind at the fragile age of sixteen when his uncle first introduced him into the dope game. Then, he was so susceptible to outside influence. Now he was like a strewing epidemic— a cancer—unsatisfied because there were still children walking around who were not under the spell of his product and there were still young black girls who he hadn't yet exploited. Green Eyes, just like most of the black drug pushers and dopefiends in Duggan had become, only exploited and took advantage of the young black girls. It wasn't like that before, they used to protect the young girls, and this was one of the reasons Ronny chose to rob him.

At first Green Eyes thought he was dreaming when he saw Ronny standing over him, pistol in his face. His senses were out of whack and his vision blurred, but not so much that he couldn't distinguish the shape of a solid figure posted in his presence. The panic was there. In both of them, it was there. But it was never truly shown. And as long as it isn't shown it doesn't really matter much.

"What the hell is this?" faded weakly from Green Eyes' mouth.

"Don't act like you don't know what the fuck this is bitch. Give us the motherfuckin' money and the dope and I might let your punk ass live." Ronny's voice thundered like he had given a war cry. He was grinning because now, for the first time in his life, he was actually in control of his destiny. He held all the authority over a man who he felt was a sellout and who felt he had higher social status, and this made Ronny feel good, like he had finally won the battle of life.

Green Eyes said nothing. He was clearly petrified but tried to appear brave. Because he was drunk he couldn't rightly match the faces with the voices. He squinted his eyes real tight and his stare went beyond the figure before him. His eyes showed no signs of his fear and he didn't flinch, not once.

"Nigga, I ain't playin' with yo sellout ass!" Ronny roared before adding: "You fuckin' Negropean."

Freddie laughed when Ronny said Negropean. Ronny then took his handgun and placed it against Green Eyes' rotund face. He directed Freddie to take over, to watch Green Eyes while he searched the house.

Green Eyes appeared dumbfounded and unsure

of himself as the two robbers switched roles. But then something had happened to him that would be impossible to explain. He began to sober up and was able to recognize his two intruders, though he said nothing. At times, the ghetto can be the producer of individuals who are heartless and envision life as a cycle, so dying doesn't really mean a whole lot to these characters because the way they got it figured is once the cycle reiterates, so will they. He folded his arms boldly, which made a threat that, in so many words, said that for a person of peasant ancestry to mess with a man of his stature would be detrimental.

Freddie politely slapped him across the face with his gun when he folded his arms. This was his reward for resistance: jaw muscles that bruised black and blue, puffed eyes, and blood rushing from his face onto a beautiful Persian rug. Freddie rolled him down on the floor like a beach ball and began kicking him passionately in the ribs. Low screams of agony were released from Green Eyes' mouth as he lay on the floor in clear discomfort.

As Freddie put his gun to Green Eyes' head Ronny came running out of the back room with a black bag full of money and dope, panting. He yelled in an outrage, "Come on! I got it! I got it!"

Freddie cocked the hammer back on his gun. No other person that night, in any part of the world saw what Green Eyes saw at that moment—the big, bulging eyes of death. After Ronny caught his breath he noticed that Freddie was going to dispose of Green Eyes.

"Don't shoot him fool! Let's go! Let's go!" Ronny panted.

Freddie abided. His body willingly left but his mind told him that the decision to let Green Eyes live would come back to haunt them.

They fled the scene within seconds, raced to the end of the block, hopped in the car, and disappeared into the thin night air. It had been a sweet robbery but unanswered questions remained floating in the air. For instance, will they now be free or will they have to live the life of a runaway? Or will they be trapped in the middle of an all-out war trying to avoid the crossfire for the rest of their time, or until somebody died? The answer to these questions, whether good or bad, seemed to be the key to their remaining happiness.

*

They were at a juke joint called Tianna's in Pals located across the tracks to the west of Duggan shooting pool when Green Eyes walked in with two of his goons, OG Mann and Baby Red, who were both as hateful towards their own women as Green Eyes was. Somebody had dropped dime that it was Ronny and Freddie who robbed him, and that somebody was a girl named Kat who Ronny slept with on occasion. She confirmed what Green Eyes already knew. They waited while the three men sat down. They continued their game until it was over and tried to leave. The men said nothing, only watched, letting them pass. Once outside they ducked around the building and ran for their lives. OG Mann and Baby Red quickly followed them outside. OG Mann was careless to the observing eyes of a witness, pulling out a black handgun, holding it with unvarying mobility, and he began firing shots with wild accuracy at the two fugitives. Ronny managed to escape, but Freddie, not so lucky, caught one in the back and was felled to the ground like a broken tree limb, suffocating in agony. In the back of his mind Ronny wanted to go back and help his friend, but he knew that if he did they both would probably die. Fifteen seconds later there were two more gunshots and Ronny knew that he had lost the best friend—the only friend—that he ever had, that it was all his fault, and he knew that he would never be able to tell Freddie's family that it was his fault.

III

His hand burrowed deep into the subsoil and seduced the likings of a small black bag. The price that was paid—his friend's death—had not been worth this small fortune.

He carried the bag under his arm, walking swiftly, gracefully, and watching his back. He skated through backwoods where copper colored mud attached itself to the back of his pant legs and shoes. Twice his right foot became stuck in the spongy soil. Henceforth, dried mud of a clay-like substance stuck to his pants so thick that it looked as if it were a part of his natural legs.

"Damn it," he cursed silently to himself while searching for his cellular phone. "I must've left my phone at that damn motel."

His only option now was to make it to a pay phone and call a cab in the now dangerous daylight, and quickly before he was noticed.

It took his frightened fingers at least twenty-three seconds before he could accurately drop two quarters in the slot. He dialed for information and the operator connected him to the Yellow Cab of Duggan. After giving the cab company the location where to pick him up he smoked at least four cigarettes. The cab arrived shortly. After being dropped off he waited outside by the overpriced Shell corner store on Frazier for the Greyhound bus. The bus did not come as quickly as the cab. The daylight faded away laggardly. The morning sky's blueness had turned into an afternoon of pale white and then into an evening of orange-red. Anxiously, he paced up and down the sidewalk wondering what could be taking the bus so long.

With every passing car, he felt a jolt of fear hit him like a lightning bolt. The jolts never deviated and he knew that they were real. He also knew that he was not in the clear yet. He stood in the red zone. This zone brought him pain, screams, dismay. Before Green Eyes gave up his manhunt, he would tear the city up.

"Pretty soon they will make their way up here if this bus don't hurry up," he said with uneasiness, knowing that he'd taken more than the money that Green Eyes and his clique used to entice their women. In all, they had gotten away with over $37,473 in money and product.

The bus arrived almost an hour late and Ronny hurriedly piled in. Without consent, his mind drifted away, away from his anatomy, away from his spirit, ascending into a blank region of space. He was living inside of a reverie.

*

…On the bus, Ronny's body shook as if the stillness and the steadiness were being replaced by uncontrollable jerks. Sweat poured down his forehead and his fingers twitched. The old man sitting next to him nudged him awake.

50

After a brief moment of puzzlement, Ronny looked around and mumbled passively, "I must've dosed off," and thanked the old man for awakening him and for not allowing him to fall deeper into the chasm of his nasty dream.

He stepped off of the bus in the not-so great Houston, Texas, but perhaps better than the city of Conroe that he had just left. He stood five feet and nine inches, dark skin, and his clothes were the same clothes that he had worn the night when he and Freddie robbed Green Eyes. The rain still poured and the clouds were darker than before. Crisp water splashed against his face, reminding him of past fears. He wiped away an imaginary tear hoarded in his left eye and beheld a city of new faces. This gave him new hope. Possibilities were infinite. His heart pounded with the excitement of still being alive and away from Duggan; now he had a chance to start all over again, a chance to create a new life.

the tree on avenue g

it stood there for as long as i can remember—
planted by the right side fence—
long, coarse, firmly rooted within the earth—
wombs opened themselves to its rigidity—
blackbirds founded a home there—

life that was beheld in a silent wind span —
indestructible by nature —
standing in a browbeaten community;
watching, silently with its pursing leaves —
the wrongs done to clarence brandley,
jeremiah milo, and the others —
but spirits, they now be, still
watched and protected by the tree
who witnessed new residents, new races,
new faces, new winters and new storms;
new mothers dying, new babies born;
standing proudly by until racial disease
came again and this tree no longer stood.

shamelessness?

All of a sudden there was this loud, crashing sound that traveled without end. It penetrated freely through the thin walls and hung in the air with a slow decline, similar to the fading tune of a dying piano note. The air was thick and hot; perhaps that is why the sound was so clear. The thickness held it and the heat magnified it. *Thump. Thump.* An unwanted sound that echoed without diminishing, holding on, perhaps to emptiness. Fading at certain corners because of the dynamics that disallow sound to hold its potency around curves. It lost its velocity but not its intensity, even if the noise was now silence. It kept coming, and once it made the bend it dipped and made this splashing sound as if it were diving into water, and you could tell that the dive had been faulty and that the diver had landed awkwardly, face first, a deathly fall; and the crash was unlimited; it held every sound that has ever been made, like a globe holding the entire circumference of the earth; there was the sound that china makes once it has shattered the stillness of silence; piercing cries of a lost child along with the loud but fading screams of a woman being held from a cliff; in the distance, the strain of a cat being hit by a car after it has just raced out into the street at night from a nearby gutter suspended in the air; in the close, it was the braying of a man caught in a fire too powerful to be extinguished; and there was the sound of death—slow, powerful, dragging. It mimicked the sounds of the suffering of slavery— the ancientness, the timelessness, the immortality—burning forever as if the sun had given it life.

When at first the sound died out and there was no longer any echo to be heard and stillness ejaculated into the atmosphere and the moon acted as if it had lost its vision, a weird feeling came over me. I sat on the edge of my bed, staring into the darkness, eyes held, at those dark and semi-solid walls, wrapping my mind around the mysterious. My room became more eclipsed as each minute passed, with each blinking of the eye, every time the slightest breath was taken, like a dark country road overshadowed by trees on both sides. When in the center of space, sound is muted and visions are unseen. The emotions that are there are imitative, like Nothing had made them exist, and feelings are sucked into emptiness. I felt everything and nothing all at once.

Time had become this angry river, leading me towards a puddle of fear, and there was no way I could reroute my path to avoid the unavoidable, so I surrendered to this fate, sadly but without regret. The atmosphere continued its shift into immediate darkness, and all around everything seemed motionless, ejected, still. I listened to the clock tick slowly away into the dark—like a shadow sitting on top of another shadow—until it was noiseless. But unlike the ticking of the clock, the shadow did not fade away, but arose again horribly from its dwelling. I re-played the scene over in my mind and it became a vivid image—the sound echoing gently in my ears—exactly how I thought it had happened, and almost mechanically, I walked towards the bathroom. There, I was joined by my mother, my sister, my cousin, eyes burning from the light, body aching from want of sleep—which is why my very movements seemed involuntary—heart skipping when I saw my grandfather lying on the floor as if he were in a casket waiting to be lowered into the ground.

Inside the recesses of space, I could hear my mother screaming hysterically: *'Go and get help! Go and get help!'* –this implored through eyes of stone. Her look was so fixated that God Himself would have been compelled to blink; and she stared with relentless focus, as if her lids had been taped to her forehead and she was being forced to watch the death of a child. Sight, the only working sense that I possessed, expressed to me what my mother's eyes were conveying, but hearing escaped comprehension: *'Go…and…get… help…Ta—r i—us?—'*

But what did it all mean? And where was I to go? And why, if God is so merciful, couldn't He just touch my grandfather and make him rise? Why did everyone have to be so dependent upon me? Who was I, but this twelve year old child?

'Go and get help'

But when I didn't move my cousin and my sister stared at me like they hated me. I was being pushed back by currents and held down by these unseen hands as if a child was being christened, and these invisible walls were closing in on me until there was little room for even my lungs to carry out their breathing responsibilities, and my body was stuck. I saw tears in my mother's eyes that I had never seen before; and I saw tears on my grandfather's cheeks that were clear and invisible. Those tears weren't there before; they had never been there; and only I could see them, with my eyes, through the tears that were there in mine but too were absent. The wrinkles in his face confused me. They formed a ragged U and made his smooth, isolated Black face look like a smile, as if he had been touched by his deceased wife's hand, as if he was happy for the first time in his life.

*

The sound was still there, lingering, like a grass stain imbedded in a white t-shirt, and my grandfather was slouched halfway in the tub and halfway on the floor and because of the floor's declivity, it looked as if he had fallen partly through. I stood above him—absorbed in the bizarre reality of the moment—scarcely hearing the words from the parting lips of the world: '*Go and get help! Go and get help!*' Sentences that were jumbled and distorted, the same way they are when they are incoherent and meaningless. Breaking and shattering—falling and disintegrating. And the sound traveled until it reached endlessness, moving slowly along its rusted axle, squeaking beyond consciousness.

It's funny how tragedies can alter relationships. My grandfather's determination to stay stuck in what seemed to me, at the time, to be a coma, in which he seemed content to remain, upset me. I wanted him to talk to me and he wouldn't speak. I wanted him to breathe and he wouldn't breathe. I needed him to smile, to pretend happiness had existed amongst us two, and he couldn't. His facial muscles were rigid; mine varied, disagreeing with every attempt at movement that was made by me, but was not still in itself. There were certain but yet unclear facial movements that I was still able to perform, all shattering from within, all unemotional.

Why did he have to do this to me? Was it out of revenge, I pondered?

'Go and get help.'

I just stood there above him wondering, lost, retarded…

…Then, every eye that has ever seen, every camera that has ever flashed, every spotlight that has ever shone, was looking at me as if to make a star out of the man who no longer wished to be seen in the public's eye.

Alienation had never been so beautiful a thing, and I sought it out, only to find that it didn't exist! I discovered that the grass has never been greener on the other side because there was no other side. That this world, this life, is all we have, and within it the unutterable existence of darkness, not Blackness but darkness, pain, tears, reality.

And I couldn't go and get help, for didn't my mama understand the shame I felt of not having a phone of our own; —and by not going, had I really done anything wrong? Was it not that my grandfather wanted his life to no longer go on? Because of the liquor I knew that he was going to die. But it haunted me knowing that I could have possibly saved his life. Sometimes, though, people may wish they were dead, but they really don't want to die. My grandfather was not one of those persons.

*   *   *

The sky had no color. Centuries of color diminished all at once, because it had no place else to go, because it was dying. It died without completion, dissolving slowly, like digested aspirin. There was nothing but darkness; this time, for the first time, absolute darkness.

Even the following day was dark in its own way. Empty and dark. Descending sunrays that belonged to the early morning were fruitless. They did not shine that bright shine that they were capable of, just sort of hung in the air like a thick fog. Thick but transparent. I knew that everything was why it was because of me. That because of my shame God punished me by taking away my grandfather's life. But could I have really saved him? The question poked at my heart. Inside I was bleeding shameless blood because the blood that was shame sweated out through my eyes, invisibly, unmarked.

Jaycie and Carl

1

Duggan, that damaged neighborhood once considered great, in the late of the year, had withered into nothing but survival. The hope and ambition of ever leaving had faded with time. The Montgomery County power structure had fooled, then flooded the Black L with their drugs, exclusion, and persecution. The black people of 2854, Pals, Duggan, and Mellow Quarters were left to carry out the rest of the destruction. Every soul became caught up in it one way or the other, regardless of economic background or education or religious affiliation. The hustle, which is what entrapped everyone, started when Duggan was merely a baby and it continued with Carl, who, as a child, thought that sports or his musical genius would get him out. The girls who refused him in grade school had all become tragic victims of the drug; Shaylyn was killed by her boyfriend—an out of towner so she immediately placed him above Carl—and dumped in a roadside ditch somewhere near Creighton Road, that family name who has a long history of bigotry. Dannie and Geena became dissipated beauty queens. Donna, once a junior high mansion now appeared a pigeon house with three small outhouses tagging along. They all thought they were fancy until the drug showed them otherwise. And then there was Crissy who later became addicted to Xanax and began whoring. She tried to rekindle what was never there for her because she felt socially above him more than she felt repelled by his 'unrefined' features in high school.

He abused some. Others he refused as they had done him. The times were changing. The streets were not as beautiful as they once were. The girls began to think differently about life. Carl wasn't that unattractive. He became curiously handsome, tantalizing the likes of the beautiful Jaycie. They were all addicted to it. Sucked in by it. Xanax. A white man's drug. It did not belong in Duggan.

2

Carl and Jaycie became intimate by association. It was a classic case of boy meets girl. Jaycie, beautiful, demanding, five feet five inches, dark caramel skin, had lost all youthfulness about living about two months before their encounter. She no longer cared about progression but accepted the pretense that addiction was hereditary. All of her aunts from the old country—Jaycie was half Asian and her mother being originally from Malaysia—had been addicted to some sort of stimulant. She eventually refused liquor because of what it did to her grandparents but instead turned to prescription pills that the people of Duggan used to keep out.

She would tell Carl, "Pills aren't as bad as liquor," a pretense she made herself believe in. She said this constantly. "At least I don't believe they are. When I drink heavily I feel sick, like the liquor's not supposed to be inside my body."

"I just think it's whatever your body can handle. You can't handle liquor 'cause your body rejects it."

"Yea and it's not like that with the pills."

Carl, for all that he lacked in composition, was quite adept in the pill selling trade. And so, when their relationship began, it was based on a lie, a lie that engulfed both participants completely until they were blindly imprisoned by both the relationship and the reason for their connection.

He stared at Jaycie, not in the eyes but in her face, and said, "I don't really like sellin' pills but it's better than sellin' crack."

"You really believe that?"

"It's the truth."

"How did we get caught up in this shit?" she asked.

"What shit?"

"This? Me and you? Pills?"

"I don't know," he frowned annoyed by the change in conversation.

Carl lived by the principle that pills were better than crack for as long as his mind lied to him. Every day it seemed they went through the same routine of saying good morning to each other, her asking for pills, him selling pills, eating half burned food, riding around the town, and then they would argue about some petty stuff.

3

Since Carl was putting nothing inside of his body nothing visible was being taken from him. There were no negative effects that he could feel himself undergoing.

"I'm good over here," he argued with Jaycie.

"No you're not Carl. You're just like me whether you know it or not."

"You trippin' girl."

His mind did not flutter, his body never fatigued or underwent sudden changes, at least not literally. For a while he ignored the mental stress through having sex, playing basketball, recording music, and by penciling his feelings in a black diary. No pain was felt.

But it wasn't always enough.

Eventually this mental stress made him see the battle of self that he was unnecessarily causing and it also made him see something else that was just a wee bit bigger than what he was. There were others who had undergone such inadequacies wherein their body seemed to be at battle with itself, most likely a result of taking, by mouth, an unnecessary amount of pills, and he knew about them, their problems, the effects that pills were having on their lives, how it made them forgetful, how it made their speech slurred, the staggered walking, the droopy eyes, fallen asleep while eating, misplacing important items, such as money, more often than not their memory, and somewhere down the line, their life. Carl witnessed all of this firsthand but continued to treat each and every one that had suffered a seizure—and the ones yet to experience that miracle—as chattel and not as the disturbed spirits that they were, probably not even as mortals who were susceptible to harm. He saw them as robots who, in exchange for a few Xanax, mechanically handed him their money, their bodies, their life, routinely slipping into darkness where the blues were being played in their minds while they rested in a brainless condition. The Xanax was like oil to them, keeping their body parts from corroding and immobilizing. He kept feeding them this injury even after near death situations, after one ran his new car into a light pole and was so spaced out that he wanted to touch the hanging electric lines because he did not understand the danger they presented, so he attempted to grab death as it jangled in front of his eyes. The same was true when another went into shock and nearly trembled his life away at that convenient store on First Street and Avenue K. And Carl continued to serve these individuals, who were inches away from dying, slow death.

These were the first two incidents. No one else had publicly suffered such a mishap. They never complained about being sluggish once on the pills. It was almost as if they revered the fact that they could get this disease and drift into that state. Carl turned his back on those who needed to be shown another way, those who needed to be denied any type of pill, giving them the opportunity to control their own destinies and taking that responsibility and blame away from himself. Once done, he was deceitfully able to come to the conclusion that he was neither moral nor immoral, but amoral, the middle ground between these two extremes, thus ridding him of any guilt.

Within days after seeing, creating, and promoting this horror, he became overwhelmed by taxing dreams, more gripping than any of the dreams he'd had before, as a child or as an adult, surrounding events that never happened but somehow seemed a part of his past. Dreams that seemed demandingly real yet were bizarre dreams that had no chance at being fully remembered once he woke from a disturbing sleep. In some of these dreams he could partially see people gathered around a town square and every one of them who was there was shaking and foaming at the mouth; but the more he thought about it, that had not been a part of his dreams at all, but something he hallucinated while woke. He wondered what these strange dreams meant because while they were being dreamt they contained some kind of acute message, like thorns poking at the layers of his subconscious with tips so dull that he could hardly make out what was happening to his body.

Maybe the messages, the hidden pain that he knew so well, that he once ignored were not ignorable after all; maybe those messages had recognizable, underlying themes and he knew what every one of those themes meant. It all had to do with power and the clout that Xanax gave him; that is what drove him on in some cases when life seemed to be at its worst; that is what guided him at night when it seemed that he would not make it through to the next morning after he thought about how meaningless his life really was. This one small white pill not only gave him importance but absolute control over peoples' destinies, all of their pretended happiness, and their valid miseries. He could make them smile by simply answering the telephone and telling them to meet him somewhere; or he could make them suffer by doing the opposite. Every dollar was a personification of his life, their life. In the wake of all this, many neglected their need to eat (notwithstanding how the pill accentuates the appetite), some neglecting the need for their children to eat. Carl was their god, neither cruel, kind, nor spiteful, nor was he a god that saw them as his creations, but a street god nonetheless. He could look into their eyes and see the hunger, the excitement, the disappointment. He created all of that and they were his puppets auditioning for roles in a very tragic drama.

4

"Close those blinds," Carl said to Jaycie, rubbing his tired eyes.

"What's wrong?" she asked.

"Nothin', just close the blinds…please."

"Okay."

"My head hurts a little and the light is too bright."

"You want something for it?"

"Nah, I'm okay."

"You sure?"

"Yea, you know I don't really like taking pills of any kind," but it wasn't a shot at her nor her addiction.

For Carl, the brightness of a Sunday morning seemed clouded rather than too bright when the curtains were pulled open. It did not possess that summer passion that once made it a memorable childhood experience. Carl and Jaycie sat in the master bedroom, blinds closed again, unhappy about this thing that kept them isolated from completeness and happiness. Jaycie turned her back, cigarette in one hand, head in the other, tears falling down one eye, welled up in the other, a sickness in her stomach. He grabbed her by the shoulders only to see her pull away. Those little actions like that created distances between them. He thought their addictions were similar. He didn't realize her diversity. His body did not require him to take the same thing that caused sickness to rid it of a nagging infection; hers did. Therefore, their addictions were not the same. The weight they carried in their minds balanced each other out in regards to blindness, pain, suffering, yet they were two addictions that were incomparable in the same respect.

Although the sun did shine brightly, there was a steady downpour of rain that kept their feet stuck in mud.

"You know that I'm addicted," She lamented when pain started its work with the glassiest eyes one could ever have imagined.

He didn't understand her addiction in the beginning, what it meant. He was still relatively in denial, making it harder for him to comprehend why she couldn't just quit.

"Why can't you say no sometimes? Is that so hard? I get depressed, I don't take nothin'."

"It's not that easy. If I didn't need 'em then I wouldn't take 'em." Jaycie looked at him solemnly. "You don't understand addiction. I've been doin' it for so long that my body cannot adapt without 'em. I get sick. You haven't seen my sickness because I take some to calm the sickness. You haven't seen that. I can't quit on my own. If I could I would. I've tried. And whether you know it or not you're addicted to 'em, too… to sellin 'em …"

"Whatever Jay." He was a bit irritated by her accusation.

At times Carl thought about walking away from it—not just the addiction, but from her too, even away from those glassy eyes—simply because that would have been easier. But then he would look into her face and see her eyes calling out to him: *take away the pain, take away the suffering*, but he did not know how. Part of that pain, part of that suffering, had been unthought; no one knew its beginnings nor its endings. The rest, the parts that did not carry any pain or suffering, but contained those glassy eyes, had definite beginnings which began somewhere along the lines when this addiction began to accelerate, but it also had no endings. These parts also opened holes in his skin which allowed an incredible feeling of pain and depression to seep in, the same way water flows through cracks in a dam, protected this pain and depression, causing his expression to be overflowed by a look of frustration that he somehow hid from the outside world. Again, he thought about walking away simply because that would be easiest. Pill addiction was foreign to Duggan. He blamed it on Jaycie's Asian side. That had to be her attraction to Xanax, nothing else. Her beauty and intimacy made him stay.

5

One Sunday, an early June, a beautiful day to behold, she stared at the blank sun rays sneaking through the tattered blinds.

"Sometimes it seems like we'll both reach our

dreams of happiness, and that dreams sometimes do come true. We just gotta keep reachin' for 'em."

"Maybe," Carl mumbled, not really in the mood for talk.

She continued after a long silence. "This can't last forever."

"No. Nothin' can, but whatever's goin' to happen I wish it would hurry up."

"Yea, so do I," she agreed.

The heavenly place that they sought continued to be pulled away from them by some external force. Carl only agreed to this statement because this, whatever it was, would not just pass.

By force of habit, or maybe something in the Sunday air caused this reaction from her, she put her ear to Carl's chest and told him, "Your heart is beating irregularly."

"What?" he asked confused.

"Your heart. It's not beating right."

"Oh. Okay," Carl said looking at her like she was crazy.

He wondered though if it was in fact his heart beating abnormally or just the imagination and the pills saying to her that his heart contained an irregular throb. These would be the days where he felt as if his heart didn't beat at all, but clung to the empty walls of his inner body, somewhere in his upper chest, somehow linked to his brain, both organs working together to keep him barely alive, which was the only reason that he needed a heart in the first place. Mentally, he would stare inside his heart and at its waste and wonder what led him to this point.

Sunday dissolved.

6

They sat on opposite edges of the bed. The air conditioner chipped away at the silence. Jaycie turned to Carl after a long silence and spoke.

"Even though we struggle, with both life and with this sickening disease, there ain't nothin' we can do but continue to fight. I feel like God has a plan for us and that all we have to do is not try to stray from that plan."

"Maybe you're right," he said.

"I think so."

"I do feel like God has a plan and that this is part of a greater plan for us both. I just don't know what yet, though. Wish I did. Can't stand not knowin' and havin' to endure all of this bullshit."

"I'm trying to trust Him," Jaycie said looking intently at Carl.

7

Days passed slowly, like they were afflicted with a deteriorating disease and the brightness within those days faltered as if it was pale skin overcome by hypothermia. With every passing day came something new, something different, varying circumstances that were always disturbing. Jaycie's attitude became climatic, changing as often as the Texas weather, influenced by her possible movement inside of a dark, filthy, concrete hell as a result of events from a time preceding her acquaintance with Carl.

Instead of giving her the normal amount he began to give her up to fifteen, even twenty Xanax on some days.

"You think if I give you more it will help?" he asked because he'd run out of suggestions.

"Yes," she agreed, deep down knowing that that wasn't the answer but succumbing to her addictive needs.

"I just want you to feel better."

"I know. I want to feel better too. I want all of this to go away."

"It will," Carl said as he handed her seven more pills.

"Thank you." She took the pills from his hand. "Can you get me something to drink?"

"Ok. What do you want?"

"A coke," Jaycie replied.

That's how it really began; that's when she first sang the blues; that's when his blues became incomparable to anyone else's blues; that's when the color of the blues lost its hue.

At a strange, spaced-out time, Jaycie whispered to Carl, "I will never leave you and I pray you do the same."

"I'm not goin' nowhere and neither are you," he replied sincerely.

But sometimes he could feel her slipping away. At a time not so strange and not so spaced-out, she insisted, "You can't place a number on life, death, pain, reality, happiness or sorrow. It is all priceless…"

"True," is all he said, not really in the mood at that particular time for deep conversation. His mind was focused on getting more money and pills.

Jaycie was headed to jail for 180 days. The day that she was to turn herself in he gave her twenty Xanax for two reasons: because she asked for them and because he wanted, for both of them, to not have to think about the separation. He did not know how in doing so the problem would be blocked from his mind, but somehow he thought it would vanish like a corpse that has gone back to dust.

There was something about the day that just didn't seem right, like the taste of a plum when it is too soft. Something about the way the sun hung in the sky that made its falling rays look like luminous tears. Then there was this incredible strangeness about the way the wind was not a direct part of the atmosphere but a force that blew indifferently into his eyes so that he could not see clearly.

When they left the apartment their feelings were lodged in between laughter and sadness. The first feeling dissolved without warning. But the sadness, as if it were a typhoon, brought in very heavy rains. In the midst of this storm is when the words disappearance and loneliness first became intimate. That is when he began to feel nauseated, like something was wedged in his throat, like a clot of blood perhaps that he kept spitting up and the clot kept rebuilding. The sun was still shining high in the sky, sitting at a slant, as if some unknown force was trying to snatch away its light. It had not lost any of its luster in the late afternoon, falling further and further behind the western half of the sky. He grabbed Jaycie's hand and she grabbed her daughter's hand as they walked to the car. Carl turned and took one last look at their apartment, frowned at the artificially dull texture, visualizing how his life would be without her.

It took everything in him to crank up his car because it would mark the beginnings of a sad journey, like when a petrified bird has broken its wing and a hungry cat stands between it and freedom. That scared him almost more than anything that he'd ever had to face in life. It was more profound than depression; more disturbing than being impoverished; more startling than death itself because this was like driving into death, or at least a death-like state. This pending separation had comparisons to a mother and her child, not a fully developed child but one still in its embryonic stages that possessed feelings. There was no way for him to continue to develop, function, or direct the formation of his life without that motherly part of him. They were taking him out of the womb even in the stages that preceded prematurity, and casting him far into the woods where even the animals are afraid to go, into the true barren wilderness.

Carl started the car, or at least something inside of him did, for he was only a mindless glob, let the windows down slightly, and backed up, trying to figure out what would happen if he did not drive down First Street towards that windswept hell, but took a more discrete path. He wondered if she would like the idea of seceding from the racist intestines of Conroe, Texas.

"You ready," he said jokingly.

"Nope," she couldn't lie, she couldn't laugh, she couldn't pretend.

75

Carl truly hated Montgomery County and everything that it stood for. It was, for black men, an imprisonment of the mind, body, and spirit. That was the black experience and Jaycie was on the verge of becoming another one of their experiments. Each fraction of a mile they passed he could feel a piece of his heart slipping into his stomach. Carl held back his tears, and so did she, possibly for her daughter's sake, but more logically to show each other that they would be alright during this upcoming absence. The tears that their eyes hid were not only premeditated lies but fear and embarrassment, stubbornness in what should have been an instance where no emotions were hidden, but an open battlefield for sadness to take aggression.

Carl parked in the visitor's parking lot where freedom continued to fade. To him, it felt like Jaycie was receiving her last burial rights and that made him feel good inside somehow, even though none of those good feelings surfaced. He did not want this to happen. Her eyes told him that she did not understand why this was happening to her or what she had done to deserve it. There were no consoling words that he could give her. A look of utter disappointment overtook his smooth, dark face and he knew that made her sadder. She kept looking in the back seat at her daughter who was eating some pecans that Carl had given her, seemingly unworried about her mother's plight; maybe that was her six year old mind telling her that if she showed little emotion, especially a dejected emotion, it'd make her mother smile. Through all of the clouds that entered his car on this non-cloudy day, Jaycie did manage to smile.

As Carl watched Jaycie's lips touch the cheeks of her mother who had met them there, then her daughter, he kept being molested by an image of being stuck in a very small space with little air. He dreaded telling her goodbye and that he loved her, aching to avoid the hardships that came with the parting. Carl just wanted it to be over, for this nightmare to run its course, for the flood waters to finally recede.

Hours after her departure, Carl continued to see that very enclosing image as it twirled in his eyes. He told himself that he was only experiencing his first hallucinations and once he turned his back he could separate himself from it. But he was already a part of the sphere and the separating never existed. The image did exist and it was as tangible as their hugs. There was nothing hallucinatory about the way her touch heightened his sense of enclosure before she kissed his cheek and whispered, "Wait for me."

And him lamenting, "I will."

Her first week in jail was a trial within itself. Freedom had been taken, but not just the ability to live within a free society; there was another freedom stripped from her. The freedom to choose, the freedom for her mind to not have to deal with reality head up all the time.

Before the first week passed, her body went into another state, like a computer with no memory still working, perhaps feeling alienated without the access of Xanax. Maybe it had been fate, or maybe something else. Either way, it caused her to have a seizure that essentially fragmented her identity, pieces that she was to never repossess.

After her release things did not necessarily get better. The addiction was still there; the struggle was still there; having to survive in Duggan with its meddlesome residents was still there.

Weekdays exuded the most sadness. She would be well for one instance and then this inexplicable sickness would overcome her appearance. It was a rare illness that did something to her face. The only way that Carl could describe the change is if he stuck his eyes in acid and came up blind. Only then would he be able to observe the minute skin discoloration, or what he falsely perceived as such, that lasted briefly and then was gone; only then could he understand why her eyes sparkled on some days and others they were downcast, yellowish eyes; and through her recognition of her need for the drug, only then was he able to understand why her body would jerk if she tried to quit on her own. Sometimes it would be such a gentle shake as to remind one of a calm ocean in the middle of the summer, and every once in a while roughly, like angry waves in the Pacific.

It happened at night on the second week of December, rampant, fear-provoking trembles. He watched over her that night as if she would disappear once he took his eyes off of her. He was reluctant to touch her, thinking that his touch would make her crumble like hard dirt.

"I'm scared. I want you to go to the hospital," He told her.

She kept refusing, claiming, "I'm scared too but I don't think going to the hospital will help."

But it was more than fear that kept her lying in that bed, searching for a sleep that did not need to be found; it was acute stubbornness. That is the unwillingness to become unset in purpose; it is an unmoving attitude; slow; stupid; established; a repetitive mental motion of unvarying opinion; million year dried up mud with a hand stuck in the center. He wanted to just yank her out of that state, out of the bed they were lying in, drag her down the stairs, toss her body in the back seat, strap her down, and take her to the emergency room forcefully like a western country overtaking a lesser developed one. She did not think of him or her child in that state because to Carl that seemed a fear that one would be willing to face. He knew she worried what her mother would think if she found out that she had been to the hospital, and that was one of the reasons that she refused to go. Carl never could value her decision. His mind would not allow him. He failed to connect the dots and make sense out of something so disconnected.

"My mama—" Jaycie started.

He screamed at her in the most respectable way possible, "To hell what your mama thank about you takin' Xanax right now! You damn near about to die or... self-destruct... or-or-or somethin'!"

"But you know how she is," Jaycie almost whispered.

Her voice was soft because it was weak because of the pills.

"Damn that, man. You need to get off that bullshit."

"You don't have to scream." Jaycie felt bad enough.

All he could think about was that she would have another seizure, there, with him, alone in that dark room and he would not know what to do. He would panic. He would freeze up. He would sweat. His eyes would become blank, and death would vanquish her just like it did his brother that autumn night at the Night Hawk club all because of his brainless reaction.

After the shaking continued to be a pester days, even weeks later, but at a lesser magnitude, as if that would somehow make it alright, Carl's sleep lessened. He stayed up and watched over her while she slept, observing her throughout the night for as long as his eyes could remain open, not wanting to lose sight of the innocence while it rested. Sometimes Carl thought that if he held her real tight he could squeeze the seizures out; then she would be safe, but he was also scared that if he wrapped up with her too close he would provoke her trembles.

His struggles with morality resurfaced, looking down on him like a conscious eye from the heavens. Carl began to blame himself for her condition—the jerking in the sleep, the detoxing, the feelings of nausea. She struggled to bring him comfort.

"I'm sorry," he said. "It's all my fault."

"You're not to blame," she told him.

She shook his head playfully. She could see in his eyes, from the gloom residing, that he felt guilt.

"This is all on me."

"It's not your fault. Hell, it ain't nobody's fault

but my own. I created this myself. They are the only thing that helped me cope with what I was going through before I met you. They allowed me to suppress feelings that were there, ready to buss. It is the only way I made it to the next day. That was the Xanax that had me feeling that way. I just couldn't take the loneliness. I only wanted to forget things temporarily. I never thought my body would become dependent." She touched his arm. "You can understand that, can't you?"

"I guess so," he said sadly.

After that initial seizure in jail she couldn't sleep most nights. Carl heard Jaycie talking one night, depressively asking, "Lord if you're with me then why won't you answer me?"

He thought it to be her seizures creeping up on her to snatch her out of his life. That's why she was looking for the Lord's actual presence that night; that's why her stomach couldn't hold any food; that's why everything that she ate loitered in her throat, causing her to consistently regurgitate. But what Carl couldn't understand is why Jaycie continued to vomit even when there was nothing there for her throw up, just the emptiness of a hard lifetime. And even through the confusion and concern of reincarnated, recurring seizures, it came to light that she might be pregnant. Every time that she threw up he pictured her throwing up a part of their child. Every time she heaved up that emptiness he pictured that same child inside her not breathing because the emptiness being heaved was its oxygen. That was not unwarranted fear that crossed his mind; that was not just concern that crossed his mind; that was a possible truth that he was a monster destroying a generation.

Section Three

Yellow Sunday

Mama dressed her in bright yellow. It was a rather recent family tradition that started with grandma; when Mama was born it was passed down to her; and now Jeanine lay claim to it.

Every Sunday, except on Easter Sunday and Mother's Day, when Mama dressed her in a costume more suitable for the day, usually pink and green, she would adorn Jeanine in a perfect matching yellow with a slight touch of a light blue of something. Her yellow skirt, which sat out overnight to get rid of the wrinkles, fitted her body like the sun did the day; her yellow stockings, yellow shoes, and a yellow and blue ribbon in her hair were the final steps to an even picture. Jeanine said it made her feel like a sunflower. She had been fond of sunflowers since she turned four and Mama finally start letting me take her into the backwoods with me to play where she picked her very first.

"But you aren't a sunflower," Mama teased. She held her head back while Mama combed it through. The strokes were soft. It reminded one of the waves in an ocean.

"I am too a sunflower. I saw it in my dream."

84

Mama held Jeanine's head back in her lap and kissed her on the forehead.

"Let me finish your hair, girl," Mama warned. When Mama seemed too relaxed and playful Jeanine would take advantage of Mama's weakness until Mama grew irritated. That's how Mama was. I don't know exactly what made her that way, to be happy for one minute and angry the next. Jeanine sat up straight while Mama jerked and pulled at the other side of her hair. "Why is this part of your hair so matted?"

"I-I don't, I-I don't know," Jeanine stumbled.

"Is this gum?" Mama sighed. The smooth strokes disappeared, replaced by short, staggered strokes that caused Jeanine to squirm and whimper. "Be still."

"Okay," Jeanine said.

But the pain created by the yanking of her hair from the comb would not allow her to sit still. Jeanine wriggled after each pull.

"I'm a pop you if don't be still."

Jeanine started to whine a little, "Mama, it hurt."

"Just let me finish now." Jeanine pulled her head back away from Mama's hold. Mama smacked her on the arm with the comb.

"Oww!" Jeanine wailed.

"Now be still so I can finish!" After that, Mama had no problem combing Jeanine's hair through her sniffles and tears. "Don't mess your clothes up with those tears now." Jeanine wiped her eyes as Mama tied the last ribbon. Mama comforted her, "I didn't want to hit you but you know we're pressed for time. Now give mama a hug and a kiss."

Jeanine obeyed and she and Mama were smiles again.

9:50 had just rolled around and Mama still hadn't cooked breakfast. We were running late. Mama seemed to be in a panic. By the time she finished combing Jeanine's hair and cooking a very hurried and burnt breakfast, I had dressed myself because I knew how Mama hated to spend too much time on both of us, then dress herself and have to fix breakfast, all in little time. I didn't wear yellow, though. It reminded me too much of hot summers and ugly, yellow teeth. The color of my clothes meant less to me because I understood that the tradition had skipped a beat, so as long as my clothes matched, I didn't complain. Me and Jeanine were only two years apart but Mama treated us very differently, as if Jeanine was three years old and not ten and sometimes as if I wasn't her daughter but a distant niece. All Mama had to do was re-comb my hair.

"I never like how you comb your hair," she hissed and I wouldn't say what was on my mind unless I wanted to be hit too.

She would redo what I'd already done, only better and with less caress than she tried with Jeanine. The yanking and the pulling didn't bother me like it did her and sometimes it seemed as if Mama would comb harder because it didn't. Mama placed our plates on the table and me and my sister gulped down what she set in front of us, half-burnt eggs, bacon, and buttered toast, without messing our clothes. Mama took our plates and I noticed she wasn't dressed for Sunday school. "Hurry up so ya'll won't be late."

"Why you not dressed, Mama?"

"I don't feel too well."

"But you don't look like you sick," Jeanine invaded.

"Nobody's talking to you, Jeanine." Mama turned back to me. "Lola," because I was named after Lola Falana, "Hold Jeanine's hand while ya'll walk down the street." She gave me five crumpled one dollar bills to put in the collection plate. "If them meddlesome people at the church ask, especially Pastor Jenkins, tell them that I was too sick to come in and I will bless them with my presence next Sunday."

"I will," I said.

Mama kissed me on my cheek and gave Jeanine a hug.

"See ya'll when ya'll get back." She waved as we skipped through the front yard.

When it was just me and Jeanine, I had to play Mama. Otherwise, Jeanine wouldn't make it to church. She stopped to pick up a few pebbles and tossed them into a nearby ditch.

"Jeanine," I started, but saw how much fun throwing those few pebbles seemed to be for her. "Make sure you don't get dirt on your dress. Mama'll be upset," I warned her.

"Do I gotta stop?"

"Nah." I didn't want to upset Jeanine before we made it to church. "Just watch your dress, okay."

She laughed and picked up a few more pebbles. She handed me some and we threw them together. The rocks looked like they were crashing jets as they flew, bounced, and skipped over the muddy ditch water.

"Okay," I said. "That's enough."

I grabbed my younger sister's hand. We continued to church, holding hands and talking about the games we were going to play when church was over. Jeanine wanted to play hide-n-go-seek because she was faster than I was; I wanted to play Simon Says because I like to make her do what I wanted; we settled on red-light-green light but since it was just two of us we were to persuade Mama to play with us. A couple of cars passed by and one of them stopped.

"Do ya'll need a ride," the man asked.

Jeanine said, "Yeah," only because she hated to walk to church unless Mama was with us.

"No thank you," I promptly added. "We alright." The car drove off rather quickly.

"But that was only Rick. We ride with him all the time when we with Mama," Jeanine said angrily.

"Mama not here so I say no."

"What you think wrong with Mama anyway? She didn't look like she was sick to me."

Thinking about it, I had to agree. Something sure was strange about the way Mama was acting this morning, even for her. And to miss church too. The only time Mama missed church is when Jeanine got run over by that car. She said she didn't feel up to it. Mama needed someone to blame so she blamed the church although the church had nothing to do with Jeanine's accident. I remember her complaining, "What kind of preacher'll let a eight-year old girl walk home by herself and get run-over by a speedin' car?" But that was over two years now and Mama was back to her steady routine of attending.

"Lola, what you think wrong with Mama?"

"I'm not sure."

"Well I know she ain't no sick like she say. Think I'm gone believe that. She can tell that lie to somebody else."

"Jeanine! Now what will Mother think to hear such talk?" We both laughed at my mock, upper-class accent.

A strong gust of wind blew from our backsides, thrusting dirt into our face. We closed our eyes and stopped on the side of the road until the wind passed, then we continued. I checked my purse to make sure I still had the five ones Mama gave me for the collection plate. They were still there.

"Race you the rest of the way." I started before Jeanine could look up.

"No fair!" she shouted as she raced after me. I took off first because Jeanine was a much better sprinter than I was even though she was younger. Mama say she got her athleticism from Pawpaw. I stopped one block away from the church so we could catch our breaths before we went inside but Jeanine kept going right passed me, laughing. She tripped over a pothole in the church's driveway and fell flat on her face. Jeanine had dirt stains on the front of her dress that I tried fiercely to brush off. I had some tissue in my purse that I used to clean her face.

"Maybe Mama won't notice when we get back." But Mama would notice, and we would both probably get fussed at for being so careless.

"She won't play with us if she's mad at us, will

she?" Jeanine inquired.

I shook my head no, thinking about the Sunday when I had tore holes in my stockings climbing trees with the kids from Twelfth Street. Mama tied three wet switches together and gave me one of her Big Mama whippings.

She kept saying, "That is not how a lady is supposed to act!"

I tore loose and shouted, "I ain't no damned lady! I'm from the ghetto, and you ain't no lady neither. We poor!"

Mama dropped her switches and stared at me for a while without moving or saying another word. Then I see water running down the sides of her face, glistening. She shook her head. "Why? Who told you to say that? Where did you get that from? Did one of them boys tell you to say that"

When I didn't answer Mama went back into the house. I stood in that same spot for a while trying to remember which questions seemed most important and the exact order. "Nobody told me to say them Mama; God showed me. Ain't that why he put us here, together, stuck in the slums, me, you, and Jeanine? Ain't that why he took away PawPaw before we knew him?"

Jeanine walked up. "Who you talkin to?"

"Mama."

"Mama?" she asked.

"Mama."

"I wanna play."

"This ain't a game!" I shouted.

"Then why you talkin' to the grass?"

I looked down at my hands and they were full of grass that I had dug up when Mama went back into the house.

The church was packed as usual with the same churchgoers and there were a few newcomers. The Greene family filled up the first two rows. Sister Browne sat next to Sister Taylor in the corner, observing every person that walked in. Deacon Troy was there with his wife, Louetta, and their six children, one of which was from another woman. Sister Annette and the gang was standing in the Amen Corner, shouting "Amen" and "Hallelujah" after almost every word that Pastor Jenkins preached. Mrs. Evans, the Sunday School teacher, sat in her usual place by her students, right behind the Elders. Me and Jeanine made our way over to where Mrs. Evans's class sat and took our seats. The newcomers were always bums or dopefiends who had felt the devil taken over their lives' the Saturday night prior unless one of the Elders from the church invited members from another church who sat in the back by the door. That way, if Pastor Jenkins tried to embarrass them by having them come up front to be saved they could just simply walk out.

We had missed Sunday school and regular church was in full blast. Pastor Jenkins had sweat dripping from his nose by the time he finished his first sermon. "God never turned his back on any man... He opened the doors to his kingdom and said... Come in... and they came... mothers and fathers... brothers and sisters... nieces and nephews... grandparents... great-grandparents... people of all ages... from all classes... from all races... But there was one group of plebeians that were too scared to approach the heavenly kingdom...And these were the outcasts... the prostitutes... the homeless... the sinful crack addicts who felt that God's decree did not concern them, though they sought salvation... And he turned to them and said... Don't be afraid my children... and opened his arms and beckoned them to enter..."

His sermons never seemed to shame the newcomers much. As long as he didn't try to have them walk the aisle for one of his traditional blessings they were okay. What they wanted was to listen to Pastor Jenkins go on and on about salvation because somehow his words chased away a week's worth of demons. And besides, Sister Annette always made the best chop beef sandwiches and potato salad and blueberry pie.

After Pastor Jenkins finished his sermon the church had its first intermission, given its parishioners five minutes to walk around, stretch, relax, socialize and listen to the choir sing soft hymns. I nudged Jeanine who had fallen asleep next to me. "I'm hungry," she said, almost too loudly.

"Well, Jeanine you gonna have to wait 'til church is over."

Jeanine stretched her arms and yawned real loud, "Can't you get me somethin' out the snack machine?"

"You know this five dollars is for the collection plate."

"But if you give them four it wouldn't matter."

"Wait 'til church is over," I hissed.

"When is church gonna be over?"

Pastor Jenkins walked by with confusion on his face.

"Jeanine is just a little hungry," I said.

"Oh, it's okay Sister Lola, I know how the little ones are when their stomach gets to talking to them."

I gave a short laugh. Jeanine didn't think it to be funny. She did not like Pastor Jenkins ever since he ratted her out to Mama when she didn't put her entire $2.50 in the collection plate, but instead told Pastor Jenkins that she needed the money for her doll's operation.

She once told me, "He ain't no pastor, he a devil."

I wasn't so sure that it wasn't any truth to him being a devil but I never said anything about it. Mama always told us that before the devil became the devil, he was an angel of heaven.

Pastor Jenkins wiped his forehead. "The intermission is just about over. Are you girls okay? Where is Sister Caroline?"

"Mama sick today," I said.

"Oh." Pastor Jenkins looked concerned. "Summer cold?"

"Yes."

"Hope she feels well soon. Will she be in next Sunday?"

"Not sure."

"Did she...well...um...did she give you...uh..."

"We have money for the collection plate."

Pastor Jenkins wiped his forehead again where perspiration, no doubt from embarrassment, had not yet fully evaporated from his first sermon. "God wouldn't like it if you were to steal from Him." He looked at Jeanine teasingly.

Jeanine said, "What God? Your God? Well your God ain't my God 'cause my God don't want no little kids' money. My God know that my doll needed an operation and that that money would've saved her."

I nudged Jeanine. Pastor Jenkins played not to hear. He motioned to one of the newcomers. A brown man walked over in a sort of glide.

"Girls, girls, I have someone I would like you to meet." The newcomer walked over. "Girls, this is Brother Love."

"Hey girls," Brother Love said clumsily.

Brother Love was a strange looking man, wasn't very tall for a man I thought. He and Jeanine favored; they both had them cute, funny shaped noses. He turned towards Jeanine. "You sho look pretty in yellow." Jeanine licked her tongue at Brother Love.

Pastor Jenkins broke in. "Brother Love is here with us today from, uh, Dallas, I believe. He is going to be joining our church, hopefully, if things go accordingly." Brother Love did nothing more but smile as Pastor Jenkins continued to throw praise his way. "Well, girls, intermission is almost over and after I finish my second sermon, Jeanine," he winked, "church will be over and you will be able to eat some of that nice food that Sister Annette and God has prepared for us today."

Jeanine, feeling like Pastor Jenkins was trying to humiliate her, protested, "I don't want none of that food. I can eat when I get home."

The people that were close enough to hear

pretended that their interests were somewhere else and when it was time everyone standing took their seats again. Pastor Jenkins headed back to the pulpit. The choir continued to sing softly under his sermon this time.

"What kind of church don't use bibles anyway?"

"Don't question the church, Jeanine," I scolded but my mind was on where Brother love was from and the people we met from Dallas so I knew I wouldn't like him.

Pastor Jenkins walked back and forth holding the microphone and looking down at the floor, still working without a bible that I hadn't noticed until Jeanine mentioned it. He hadn't allowed a bible in his church ever since I can remember so it never occurred to me to be odd. I wasn't exactly sure what religion this church celebrated since one had never been outright professed, but it was something like Methodist, Baptist, and Episcopal pressed all in one. Alongside my reflections Pastor Jenkins continued, never quoting biblical scriptures or using *-eth* at the end of his words like preachers tend to do for emphasis. Jeanine always found that to be strange. When she read the bible at home she would always ask me about strange words like speaketh and thee. She had read many bible stories and found them very amusing, not true, but amusing, but Mrs. Evans never taught any of them in her Sunday school class. It was always allegories about drug dealers, junkies, prostitutes and bums in our neighborhood, a leading up to the tales that Pastor Jenkins would tell in his sermon. Pastor Jenkins had banned the use of bibles some time ago when he was a member of the A&E church because he figured God had not actually written the bible but man that claimed to be some sort of prophet, so he too could declare prophecy and preach about things that people know are real.

"The bible has too many fantastic stories," he would always say. "The only sea that departs in the ghetto is the sea that separates the rich and the poor."

He started his very own church with his own religion a few years back, New Wave House of the Lord, which was not exactly a real religion, even Jeanine could see that, but had enough followers from the old church, including Mama, for him to carry out his beliefs. One thing Pastor Jenkins did not do is give people divine hope. When a member of his church could not pay their bills he did not tell them that God would take care of everything. He took care of it himself and made sure they knew it was his doing. In return, the beneficiary would have to work at the church and his house for two weeks doing small, non-exhausting jobs. I think Pastor Jenkins to be a crook though, but I guess that's with all preachers, are at least most of them in our hood.

I heard his voice suddenly: "Yesterday, I was coming from the grocery store...buying some...um...some of that good, healthy, keep your body right food...high priced items that the good Saviour has allowed me to get so I can...uh...uh...keep spreading the word of the New Wave..."

The church was quiet as Pastor Jenkins broke into his story. Sister Annette remained in her seat. The choir kept humming, only this time each member of the choir took turns humming solos. Jeanine was fidgety, turning around every so often to tell me that the man that pastor Jenkins called to meet us was staring at us. I made her sit down and look forward.

He continued: "...You see, New Wave's not just a religion, it's a way of life..." He sat down next to his podium. "Brothers and Sisters, as I was leaving that grocery store a man walked up to me, dirty, smelly, hungry, weak...a junkie man that has disowned and has been disowned by the Saviour, by the community...See, see, now I knew this man was a junkie without asking him...No, no, I didn't have to ask him...I could see it in this man's face...through the filth...the coughing...His arms were the arms of a junkie...his clothes were the clothes of a junkie...his shoes were the shoes of a junkie...his smell was of a junkie smell...his walk was the walk of a man who had not been sober in days..."

Pastor Jenkins looked around at the faces of his congregation. He saw that he had their complete attention, well, all except for me and Jeanine. They were too eager to see where his story was headed to space off but I knew Pastor Jenkins's stories never had a point.

He resumed. "...His eyes were red from lack of sleep...I asked this man did he believe in the Saviour and his fatigue did not allow him to answer...But good people this man's eyes told me that he had given up faith in the Saviour...his only Saviour was crack...This man did not ask me for mercy...he did not ask me for shelter...he did ask for nourishment...He wanted money, lots of it, to buy the high priced dope...But I told him my money went on these bags of food to feed my family and if you want to come and have dinner with my family I will happily take you in but I will not give you money for CRACK..."

He put a strong emphasis on crack that sent a few dozen Amen's through the church.

Pastor Jenkins continued making a connection with high priced drugs and high priced food in his sermon somehow until he figured he had struck a nerve with the newcomers, then the collection plate was passed. Deacon Troy gave the last prayer and church was dismissed. During this time I saw Brother Love and Pastor Jenkins talking away from everyone else. I couldn't make out what was said but I saw Brother Love hand Pastor Jenkins an envelope and leave. He was the only one to leave. Everyone else went into the kitchen for Sunday dinner. Pastor Jenkins talked to me and Jeanine for about thirty minutes about what he was going to preach about next Sunday and acted as though he wanted our opinions. I told him that his plan sounded fine, for Jeanine was getting irritated and I wanted to both get her home and to get Pastor Jenkins smelly breath out of my face.

On the way home Jeanine walked extremely slow. I told her, "Hurry up, Mama'll be worried if we don't get home soon."

"What she got to be worried about? She the one that didn't have to go to church and listen to Pastor Jenkins talk about people. I wish I was grown so I wouldn't have to go either."

The sun shone brightly, making Jeanine's yellow dress a blur in the afternoon.

"That Brother Love was a funny lookin' dude, huh?"

"He looked kinda like you," I teased. Jeanine frowned. Her face was so young that it barely made wrinkles. "I mean, ya'll got them same funny noses." I squeezed Jeanine's nose tenderly and she jerked away. "Cute noses," I added.

"Yeah, well ya'll got the same face." Jeanine took off towards home with me chasing not too far behind. Mama was sitting on the front porch waiting for us with a man standing next to her. "Who that?" Jeanine asked.

"I don't know."

"Hope it ain't Pastor Jenkins come tell Mama another lie 'cause if it is I'm a hit his car wit' a rock."

"That's not his car."

"Well, whoever car it is he bet not be tellin' Mama nothin' about church 'cause I ain't did nothin'." Jeanine lips shook with fear.

"I'll let Mama know you ain't done nothin' to nobody. Don't worry." I gave her a big hug but I don't think it took away her fear. We walked into the yard with caution and saw that it was only Brother Love.

"What he doin' here?" Jeanine said lowly so that Mama couldn't hear.

"I don't know."

Jeanine ran up to Mama and gave her a kiss, licking her tongue out at Brother Love who found it amusing.

"Did you enjoy church?"

"It was okay Mama. It was hot in there though. I wish you would've been there. Rick tried to give us a ride to church and Lola made us walk." She looked at me with piercing eyes, then at Brother Love. "What you want wit' my Mama?"

Mama kept her head low but I could tell something wasn't right with her. Her voice was shaky when she talked to Jeanine. She never once looked up, not at Jeanine or at me. Brother Love just stood and smiled nervously while Mama tried to justify his being there. "Jeanine, honey...Lola...this here, this is Mr. Love...I mean Ronnie Love...He is...this right here is ya'll's daddy sweetie."

"Who?'

"Y'all's daddy."

"I thought you said daddy died at his job when you was pregnant with Jeanine?" I asked, confused.

"No, honey, daddy's right here."

"He don't look like my daddy." Jeanine said.

"That's because you were too young to remember how your daddy look, baby."

"Why he here?"

Both Mama and Mr. Love's eyes widened. Mama wiped her eyes repeatedly though there was nothing in them.

"So we can be a family again. Wouldn't you like that?" She wiped her eyes again.

"I don't know. Can we trust him. You always told me not to trust love 'cause it ain't real and his last name Love, and Mama you said you was happy when daddy died," I said.

Brother Love spoke for the first time since church. "Smart girl." He winked at me. "Lola, Jeanine, things gonna be different now. Daddy's back and this time I won't leave my three favorite girls to fend for themselves. I'm doin' better now and I, I know it ain't no excuse but that's why I left. I needed to get myself together. Just didn't think it would take as long as it did. Got a good payin' job and was finally able to get transferred back home." He grabbed Mama and gave a forced laughed.

Right off, Mama seemed to enjoy having daddy around. It took Jeanine a few days to accept his being there. It still surprised me how easily and quickly she accepted Ronnie into her life when at church, just a few days ago, she was complaining about how much she hated all the newcomers that ever came to church on Sunday and when Pastor Jenkins introduced us to Brother Love she rolled her eyes at him. Mama I could understand. She had been raising me and Jeanine alone and I never seen her with a boyfriend, never seen her happy before. Her, Ronnie and Jeanine—the family—were lost in nostalgia. They stayed up half the night listening to Ronnie tell stories of he and Mama's past and of his travels and how different things would be now. I tried to sleep but every time I closed my eyes I saw images of me becoming an outsider. It was a little past three when Jeanine climbed into the bed that we still shared, in high spirits.

"Daddy say he gone get me a bed and fix up that other room so I'll have my own room." She knew that I wasn't asleep somehow, probably through her newfound excitement.

"That's nice."

"He say he gone get you that scooter that you been askin' Mama 'bout too."

"That's nice." I rolled over so not to face Jeanine as she spoke of these miracle things.

"What you mean that's nice?" Jeanine shoved my body causing me to nearly fall off the bed. I sat up and looked at my little sister hard, trying to make her see the anger in my eyes through the darkness.

"Jeanine, what do you know about this man?"

"Huh?"

"What do you know about Brother Love?"

"I know he my daddy."

"How do you know that?"

"'Cause he and Mama said so."

"But where has he been?"

"I don't know."

"If he really cared he wouldn't a left us. Just 'cause he say he our daddy don't make it so."

"I'm goin' to sleep," Jeanine said.

"Why? Because you don't wanna hear what I got to say? Because you know I'm right? Jeanine, what is it 'bout this man that you like. You actin' like Mama. I can't blame her 'cause I always knew she wasn't complete. But you? What happened to your toughness? What happened to you never wantin' to know who your daddy was 'cause you had me and Mama? What happened to never carin' for a man who would leave a little child alone wit' its mama, even if it was through death?"

Jeanine drifted off to sleep under the weight of my questions. At daybreak I took her into the backyard for a game of hide-n-go-seek, only I wanted to talk to her some more about about Ronnie.

"Who gone be it?" she asked when we got out there.

"Nobody. I didn't bring you out here to play. I wanna talk to you about Ronnie."

I could see the disappointment overtake Jeanine's face. We sat near the fence away from the house. I brought out some snacks with us to keep Jeanine's interest. She was reluctant to talk at first but when I promised her I'd give her my five dollar allowance on Monday she opened up like a trusting heart. She told me all about Ronnie, as much as she could remember, his life since he's been away, his life with Mama before I came, and that once, while living in Baltimore, he'd been shot. Jeanine eyes got real big when she explained that part of the story, adding more detail almost certainly to the original story.

She told me, "Daddy also say he got a case of the sleepwalkin'. Been wakin' up in different parts of the house. Mama don't know it 'cause he get up before her and get back in the bed wit' her 'fore she wake up. She know about his sleepwalkin' though, from before; she just don't know he still doin' it."

Several Sunday's later Mama did not wake us up for church. I found her in the kitchen standing by an idle stove. "We not goin' to church, Mama?" I wiped the sleep from eyes. Mama was thinking of cooking breakfast. She had her back turned towards the stove. "Mama?"

"I heard you, Lola." Mama kept her back turned away from me. "You hungry? We have bacon, pan sausage, eggs, grits, biscuits, and juice." Mama cut the stove off. "We won't be goin' back to church for a while." She grabbed three plates and three glasses from the cabinet. Mama beamed yet her eyes seemed frightened, like they had seen destruction but could not tell anyone of its coming. She set the table and called for Jeanine. "Jeanine! Come eat honey."

"She still sleep, Mama. Want me to wake her."

"Nah. Let her sleep."

I noticed that Ronnie was not standing beside Mama singing in her ears like he had done since he been here.

"Where Ronnie?" I hadn't yet been able to call him daddy.

"He went to get you that scooter you wanted. He'll be back in a lil' while."

Ronnie had made true on all of his promises since his return. He had gotten Jeanine her very own bed to sleep in and fixed up the other room for her; Mama had new furniture in the dining room in case she wanted to invite over company; and now my scooter! But I still couldn't bring myself to accept him into our lives.

"After you finish eatin' I want you to take a bath and get dressed. When your daddy comes back you can go play outside in the backyard with your new scooter. I don't want you in the street until you learn how to ride it well enough to."

"Okay, Mama." I ate hurriedly so that I'd be

ready when Ronnie came back without asking about church again.

"You better slow down or you might choke."

"Just excited, Mama."

Ronnie walked in before I finished breakfast. "How's my little girl?" He rubbed his hands through my hair.

"Stop it Ronnie!" Mama pushed Ronnie away from me.

"Caroline!" If it wasn't for the wall Ronnie would have fell to the floor. "What's the matter with you, Sweets?"

"What's wrong, Mama?"

"Nothing, baby. Just hurry up and finish and go bathe." Mama barked.

"I'm done, Mama." I lied.

"Leave your plate. I'll get it," she said.

I headed towards the bathroom but stopped around the corner to listen to Mama and Ronnie's conversation. "What'd you do that for, C? Why'd you push me like that?"

"You know why."

"Are you still on that? I told you what that was. How long you been knowing me and my condition? I can't help it but I don't mean nothing by it."

"Yeah, I know what you said you lyin' ass bastard."

109

In the tub I wondered what it was that Ronnie had done that had Mama in such a stir.

"Your scooter's out back," Mama yelled in. "After you get dressed go out back and play."

It was nearing noon when Jeanine finally got out of bed. She sat on the back step and watched as I fell off the scooter again and again.

"You wanna try?" I asked her.

"Nah. It look too hard."

"This is how you learn how to ride it lil' sis. You have to fall before you get good at it."

"I don't wanna fall."

"You must not gone ever wanna ride it alone?"

"Not if I gotta fall in the grass like you keep doin'."

Jeanine never had a problem with falling and sprawling out in the grass before. She'd changed since Ronnie's coming, become more prissy, more less like my tomboyish sister that I knew and loved and more like my girly sister that I was starting to dislike.

"Well, when I get good enough on it I'll let you ride on the back. Deal?" I told her.

"Deal."

Jeanine slept with Mama that night. Me and Ronnie stayed up late watching TV and talking. It was the first time that we'd been alone, just he and I, since his return. I found him to be charming and a willing talker.

"Thank you for the scooter."

"No problem, baby. You know, if you're good and keep gettin those A's in school there will be many more presents, many more." I think Ronnie smiled a lot because he was still nervous around us and smiling allowed him to get through awkward moments.

"What was wrong wit' Mama this mornin'?"

Ronnie lit up a cigar. "Lola, Lola. You know you was named after Lola Falana? That was Big Mama's favorite singer and actor. My mama wanted to name me after Lola Falana but I came out a boy so before she passed I promised her that my first born girl, I would name her Lola. Named your sister after Big Mama." He took a puff of his cigar. "You know you cried a lot as a baby. Drove your Mama crazy some nights. I would sit up wit' you in my arms, rockin' you until you fell asleep. You never really wanted a bottle much, just for someone to hold you. In fact, you was the only baby that I've ever known that didn't put everything in its mouth. Thing is, your mama wanted too much. More than what I had and more than what I could give her. I never wanted to hurt you or your Mama or Jeanine. Believe that honey, and no matter what they say, I would never knowingly hurt my girls."

"I believe you." I didn't comment towards his love gestures or ask him again about Mama because whatever happened that had her so upset he felt he couldn't tell, or shouldn't tell.

Summer ended without another word of what happened that Sunday morning that made us stop attending church. It was nearing time for school to let back in. Ronnie bought us new clothes for our first two months of class. I was entering my freshman year in high school and Jeanine was entering the seventh grade. He promised and made good on his promise that he would drop us off and pick us up each day, give us lunch money and help us with our homework. I had started to fall under his spell while it seemed mama and Jeanine were falling out. "I'm kind of glad that Ronnie is here."

"If you so glad then you have him!" Jeanine was nearly in tears.

After we'd done our homework and eaten, at night, once, right before Halloween, I could hear Jeanine in the next room talking in her sleep. She was yelling at something to leave her alone. "Stop boy. Stop boy. Stop it. That hurt."

I rushed into her room and cut the lights on.

"Jeanine! Jeanine! Wake up!" I shook her hard. "You was dreamin'. It's alright, I'm here wit' you."

Jeanine looked so scared. I could tell that she did not believe that it was alright. Whatever she dreamt, I could not protect her from. "What was your dream about?"

"It was nothin'. Will you sleep in here wit' me tonight?" she asked.

"Yeah. Sure."

"Keep tha lights on."

I watched over Jeanine while she slept that night, watching out for her dream if it came back. Sometimes she would toss and turn in her sleep so I had to keep putting the covers back on her. Morning was hesitant to come. I had fallen asleep in the corner where Jeanine woke me. "Thanks for sleepin' in here wit' me."

"Jeanine, while you was sleep you kept knockin' the covers off of you. I saw that mark on your leg. Where did it come from?"

"I don't remember."

"Did it have somethin' to do wit' your dream?"

"I don't remember."

"What do you remember?"

"Fear."

Ronnie and Jeanine had went to the grocery store right after sunset so me and Mama sat out on the porch to wait for their return. It was a beautiful night, one that I wished could last forever.

"Mama, have you seen Jeanine's scar?"

"What scar?"

"The scar that's on her thigh, Mama. She told me how she got it," I lied.

"She did?"

"Yeah."

"I didn't know she had a scar." I could tell Mama was lying.

"Why did ya'll try to hide it from me?" I asked.

Mama looked up into the stars. "It's so many. Have you ever wished upon a fallen star, Lola? I used to. My mama told me that fallen stars brought good luck. I've seen so many fallen stars but never the good luck that is supposed to come with them."

Jeanine showed fear towards Ronnie and hatred towards Mama. On the weekends she stayed in her room and watched cartoons all day. Sunday mornings she would dress for church in her yellow outfit knowing that she wouldn't be allowed to go. She'd put on her yellow dress and yellow ribbon like Mama did and pretend to be at Sunday school with Mrs. Evans. In her make-believe Sunday school class, Mrs. Evans taught her how to make evil disappear. Before Ronnie fixed up the other room me and Jeanine would sit in there and wonder what it would be like to be rich.

But Ronnie came and took all of that ugliness out

of the house. During this process of prettying up came a much deeper ugliness. Jeanine sat Indian style next to her dresser. She had some construction paper set out in front of her. On it was a picture of her and Ronnie lying next to one another. Both she and Ronnie had knives pointing at her thigh. I picked up the drawing and looked at it for a moment. Jeanine was laughing. "I forgot to draw you and Mama."

I sat down beside her. "It's okay baby sis'." Something reflected in Jeanine's eye, some sort of newborn sadness. "What made you draw this picture."

"Shhh. Mrs. Evans 'bout to come back in. She don't like it when you talk durin' Sunday school. Sit closer to me." I moved closer. "Hold my hand. Now, I'm a play like I'm Mrs. Evans but I'm a sit right here, okay."

"Okay."

"Class, today we have a special visitor. Everyone welcome Miss Lola." We both clapped and welcomed me to Sunday school. "Jeanine will be leading our class today so everyone be quiet because Jeanine now has the floor." Jeanine let my hand go. "I have to stand up now." She stood up and sat on top of the dresser. Mocking Pastor Jenkins she began, "Class, today I have a story to tell...One about a man and a girl..." I thought she was going to laugh when she looked up at me smiling. She jumped down from the dresser and sat back on the floor. "Mrs. Evans said Sunday school is over."

"Over?"

"Yeah." She smiled. "Now let me tell you 'bout my scar." Jeanine looked at my eyes intensely. I nearly shivered. "Ronnie made that bite on my leg. Mama think he done it on purpose. I told her he didn't but she won't believe me. She think I'm coverin' up for him 'cause he been gone so long. She think I don't want him to go again but I don't care if he go or stay though. I didn't feel it while he was doin' it, you know, from the Nyquil I took for my cold. He done it so softly I guess. Daddy say he don't know what happened, that he just woke up beside me with his shirt in his hand and Mama hittin' him with the broom, you know 'cause of his sleepwalkin' disease they never told us about. That's not why Mama and Daddy don't sleep in the same room no more, because of me. Mama say she don't love Daddy. She was just happy when he first come back."

She faded off. I could see that Jeanine had been keeping this a secret because she didn't want to ruin the family's happiness but it wasn't her fault, didn't seem like Ronnie's fault neither; seemed like Mama was ready for it to just be us again.

"Mama's happiness already gone, Jeanine."

Her nightmares would not go away. I could hear her through the very thin walls every Sunday night yelling like she was being attacked. There was no way for me to save her from her sleep. Sleeping in the same room with her sometimes helped a little but we still dreamed separately.

The household stayed quiet. Ronnie spent extra hours at work even though he wanted to be with the family. I thought he was going to leave again but his past mistakes would not allow him. He wanted to; it was in his face. He maintained his innocence throughout but Mama was stubborn. She did not trust him. Mama made herself believe, because her love for him was not love at all but hate that she thought was love, that what she saw was Ronnie killing Jeanine even though Jeanine did not even believe it. Ronnie added walls and a ceiling to the back porch and moved his things out there. We were not allowed to visit him nor talk to him when Mama was around except for Sunday dinner's when we all sat at the table like we were a happy family. Jeanine no longer dressed up in yellow and made like she was attending church. The past seven months had showed her something else in life. It took away her childhood. We were not as close as we used to be; she and Mama were not close anymore; and Ronnie was a loner. I started sneaking out there to talk to him. I knew he loved us and because of this love he could not be with us.

"Lola. I don't know what happened that night but I promise that I would never do anything to hurt my girls. All I know is I was walking in my sleep and I woke up in the bed with Jeanine bleeding and your Mama screaming. She was hitting me in the head, trying to kill me I believe. There was me half naked..." He cut off. His eyes were red from crying. His words seemed truthful enough. I hugged him for the first time since his return. He was reluctant to accept this warm gesture because of Mama. Once he conceded he burst into tears. "You better go before Caroline catch us."

I left Ronnie in that dark part of the house alone with a heavy heart and a dark conscience. Before I closed the door I turned to him and whispered, "Ronnie, if you wanna leave again I won't blame you."

Amber

7

Amber was only seven when she witnessed it. The late afternoon sun brushed against her pale white face. The state labeled her insane afterwards, when the sun touched her cheek. Authorities tossed her pale body in a room and forced her to remember. Her brain did not register the events. Her soul drifted away. She grew up in spite of her limitation, her beauty clinging to emptiness, her mind to broken patterns. The wind whispered into her ears, a sweet sound like the one sung by the bittern raven when the day relaxes. Amber hadn't shed a single tear since that day. She stoned her heart against life.

Her father looked like a worn out sun, pale skin glistening from sweat. White worn out sun that time forgot. He loved his wife once, deeply, but unproven suspicion under the influence of liquor knows no limits. He stood over her body, dribbling at the mouth like a mad dog, twitching eyes. She was positioned on her knees under a pecan tree. Amber watched under a pained sky. Pleasant blue and shedding sky where love yearns for appreciation. He had condemned his wife as a no-good, cheating whore; said she had to depart this life. She only gazed into the repressive Texas sun. Her voice was low with the wind. Her face remained dry. The sun continued to brush their faces with its false mercy. Beautiful young world calling out, extending its golden hand...missing spirit of the universe. His hands wrapped around her neck. Powerful bruised hands, full of rage. She turned colors from the pressure. A bright red, then a dismal bluish-red. Saliva dripped from her mouth right before the cherry blood. The color rushed from her deadened face. The sun's rays cringed away from her white reflection. He let her body fall to the earth. Her eyes unclosed. Her lips unmoving.

Amber stood under the sky, clear liquid falling from her doubtful grey eyes.

"It had to be done honey. You understand don't you?"

Only the sky knew if Amber understood.

"I understand daddy."

He touched her shoulder with his terminative hand.

"You want tell nobody will ya honey?"

The sun had intermingled its rays with her tears; a blank rainbow flowed into her face.

"I won't tell nobody daddy. I promise I won't."

"That's a good little girl. Now go play in your room until daddy come back in."

It was a sullen room. She peeped just behind the tattered curtain, following her father as he ambled into the shed. He came out with a worn shovel and rusty hoe. The ground needed to be watered around the tree. He removed his wife's existence from rumors of her 'satisfying' the many men she sometimes entertained in the back of Mama J's;

yet, he spent his weekends inebriated trying to entice young hookers of all races. Amber's underdeveloped body filled the window. Her father looked up and waved at her before covering the hole that he had dug.

15

Look into her grey eyes, her empty eyes where her mother's soul floats. A clear emulation of existence that once was. She bathes in paradigms while sucking on southern pine needles. She is not her mother.

Amber never learned to cook to a man's standards. It upset her father. When he came in from a twelve, sometimes fourteen hour shift down at the old lumber yard on Silverdale he went straight to the kitchen table made of logs that he'd taken from his job in the late night and demanded his eats. He deserved that as a man, taking care of the household, regardless of what he did to her when the sun drowned. His beer always tasted the same. Nasty but effective. His intake determined the taste of Amber's cooking. Sometimes she would ask the neighbors to help prepare. They didn't like intervening much; didn't want to disappear like Amber's mother had done. No one talked about that openly; they only whispered it. The atmosphere quelled it. Amber could sense the discontent in their eyes. She stopped asking. She shut a second door around her heart. Like she had to do with her mother.

The sun burned out slowly in the dark. In the beginning, any time she overcooked the food her father beat her. Sometimes the beatings were only verbal. Amber set the plate in front of him loosely, nervously. It banged on the table, the hard glass on that raw wood. He looked at the over-cooked pieces of chicken. It smelt liked fire. Amber's lips were trembling. But her father, too inebriated to react, took another swig of his beer and fell asleep in his plate.

The passing out did not take away the nightmares. Her father stares into her grey eyes, her empty eyes that reflect nothing. Her eyes are a nightmare.

The other residents that lived down the hill knew nothing, only assumed what the universe already knew. Rumors began to circulate, reaching the lower part of Duggan that floods by the branches. The police investigation eight years prior had been only one of questioning in which they were told that the wife had run away with some sleazy man she had met at Mama J's. The Conroe Chronicle ignored the story. Both parties privately believed that any white family living in Duggan was not part of the greater whole anyway. They were outcasts, and rightfully so. What could they contribute to the booster club or to the advancement of places like River Plantation and Lake Conroe? Not that those places were any good to the land. But the father and mother were both white, just real poor, passing for black poor as the county officials liked to put it in their private meetings. That made Amber passing for black to them also.

The state took Amber from what the school nurse had said about her psychological state, not because of her missing mother, but for research. The bulging ground of spiritual love by the tree went ignored. When the sun closed its eyes Amber would sneak out to the tree for revocation. She became part of the bulge. She melded her wretched soul with the earth.

…Apparently, Amber wasn't very attractive, as a child or as an adult. The teenage boys did not lust after her like they did other girls of her age. But she had some beauty somewhere. The only man to love her emotionally or physically was her father. He evolved into her nightmare. It began the day after the first bad meal, about a month after she returned from Cleveland Store, exactly 46 days after he buried her mother, after the neighbors refused help, that he played doctor with his daughter, complaining of stomach pains. She did not want to end up like her mother. He told her the kisses were for being a good little girl. The touching was part of her surgery to make her grow into a woman. Later he said it was to remove the bad food. So when she became pregnant they found a willing physician to abort the child in exchange for a second game of doctor and a nominal fee. The father went back to work; Amber went back under the tree. The sun continued to brush against their sullen faces.

31

"The doctor will see you now, Ms. Miller."

The voice of the nurse reached her thoughts though she was mentally somewhere else. She felt indifferent to getting rid of another child, her diseased child, her father's child, the almost all black child based on its class. It had become routine, like the sun that closed its eyes on her all the time. The procedure ended fairly quickly. She learned how to harden herself by blanking her memory till it was over. She didn't think of it as a child, but as a jumble of clay that had to be removed from her body. If she kept it, it would not laugh and giggle like other infants since it wasn't human. She had to do what was right and proper. Besides, after so many abortions her body could not carry a baby full term anyhow.

She slumped back as the abortionist took her under. When she came back from her swoon she was once again without child. This time she felt different. Her game of doctor prior was entered with shame, even with the numbing drugs. Her insides hurt. But it was worth the 50% discount.

...Her room was dark. She pasted red construction paper over the window. Her white shield, the skin that was supposed to be her gift, failed in protecting her. This neighborhood protects no color. A few outsiders, similar in class to the earliest immigrants, experimented on living there. They were hoping to find value in the land like they did in The Woodlands, then push the natives out and rename the neighborhood after some man whose existence is debatable; they realized they could not settle Duggan. The land only offered despair to those whose only wish was to plunder. She often wondered what would have happened if she'd let her first child live, if the game of doctor would have stopped? She knew the answer. It wasn't a wish, only a curiosity. She told herself it was because of her destitution that she couldn't have that first child. When she got herself together she would have a family outside of her father, nice house, husband and all. History repeated four times.

At thirty-one Amber still lived with the man that took her mother away. She never left home or had an outside relationship. She hated men's privates from what her father did to the point that she kept her feelings toward them suppressed. They were all the same. Wife killing, beer drinking bastards. Dust tracks on a railroad, she would leave them as they lay. She prepared dinner for her father that night after her last abortion, same as always. She was in pain. It was his last week at the lumber yard. He would be retiring soon so he demanded his meals be better prepared. He, like his daughter, gave up the idea of finding another woman to take the place of his 'estranged' wife. They melded into a strange relationship. The flowers along the edges of the house peaked under all suns. She brought some into her dark room. Within two days they were dead. The flowers outside were looking more like country bushes than flowers after their initial blossoming. The food she prepared was still burnt. It was still chicken. It still smelt like fire. That night he came back into her nightmare. It was too soon after the abortion. She was not asleep. He tried to give her a fifth but he remained flaccid. So he did like little children do with their clothes still on. It was Amber's first tears since that day. Maybe she wanted it this time. She told herself she didn't.

Her body ached all over.

*

Unattended shrubs had nearly concealed the house. No one saw Amber and her father much. They went to supermarket at night, washed clothes in their back yard using a washboard. Whispering pines of a woman going into the house arose. They believed it to be the mother. The shrubs grew into weeds.

Amber had found beauty within herself. Pain dissolved. She used it to create contentment. The sun brushed her face in the dark. She woke her father up for his insulin shot.

"You holdin me too tight, honey," he muttered.

"Be still." He couldn't be still.

"It ain't time for that damn shot."

He saw death when he stared into her empty grey eyes. He didn't have the strength to jerk away from her grip. He left it out there in the fourteen hour a day, thirty-five year lumber yard. The needle went into his vein. Amber closed his eyes. He would not see afterwards like her mother. She put him next to his wife under a hidden moonlight. Dirt enclosed, shovel and hoe with him, his body would never touch her soul again. There would not be a fifth.

The ambulance showed up late when reports went in that the house had been set afire. By the time they arrived the house had lost its structure. It could not be saved. Some of the smoke appeared to be hants, the images of a man and woman, daughter and child. They all saw it so it couldn't have been a delusion. They agreed. Angry white souls finding each other in death. No one saw Amber again. She meld into the ashes.

Lovely

She was not the prettiest girl. Men were still pained at not knowing the inside of her heart. Their sorrow seemed cyclical. The little boys' hearts were filled with curiosity. It was impossible for many of them to smile inside since they meant so little; they could not get to her. Only hope to grow into her touch. Grown and young men daydreamed of deflowering her. Clouds sometimes passed over their sun without blocking its rays or its warmth. The sun's duties passed by days unharmed. The radiance in the stars that orbited their galaxy was not always faint with white darkness. She had this effect on a number of the boys in Duggan. Lovely's birth certificate said she was white because her father was white. Her skin was a smooth brown like her mother.

*

The moon she saw last night was beyond human description. It sat so low in the sky with its beautiful, carroty hue while she watched as very thin clouds attempted to cover up its brilliance...Southern moon-child from an interstitial world of beauty and unprettiness.

...As a child, she didn't associate with the little black boys from Duggan; their hellos were often greeted with sighs. She saw them as classless, ignorant fools. They lived in a cycle of birth, hopelessness, oppression, drugs, jail, and death. Her black mother told her that her underlying whiteness would shield her against the black cycle. Her relationships were with supposedly ambitious white boys who attended the high school; even perpetual foreigners got to feel Lovely's sensation. They all treated her the same way. Loved her, then made love to her. It was Lovely's doing really. They hadn't exploited her as much as she took advantage of their gullibility. Her name resonated in the school hallways from jealous girls. The cafeteria lunch line was a meeting ground for gossip. Girls wrote nasty things about her in the bathroom stalls. Girls who didn't garnish the same attention as Lovely, who didn't have the duality she had. Some of these girls were all prettier than Lovely; some were not; many of them were full-blooded black; their beauty, Lovely was taught, was trivial.

She was subjectively promiscuous at an early age. She picked the boys most susceptible to her cruel kindness. Her interest for them usually waned after two weeks. For them it was the best two weeks of their teenage life. She left them devastated. One boy hanged himself from his bedroom window when Lovely stopped answering his phone calls. Tied a rope to his bedrail and leaped from the second floor of his parents' house. Another boy stalked her, passively, unsuccessfully, until his resolve led him to the muddy banks of Blue Lake where she first let him taste her water. Lovely only sighed. She was intimate behind the gymnasium the very next day with an underclassman.

...Lovely wasn't to blame for her snobbishness entirely. Her personality had been tainted by the favoritism in her upbringing that comes with being half white.

Her mother warned her, "Stay away from the no-good black boys. And that little black boy who you sometimes walk to school with ain't nothing but trouble," her mother said. "Use him for protection, for changing your tires," she warned. "But don't ever let him see your womanhood."

She told Lovely of how the only black man she

had ever loved had broken her heart. He had blamed the miscarriage on her. He left her homeless. Lovely's father did the same. Left her at the hospital right after the baby came because Lovely's skin was too dark for his parents' liking. They tolerated the mother's pregnancy in hopes that the child came out fair. Lovely's father was not there for the naming. The mother did not hate him. She looked at her baby with her beautiful brown skin and her father's Nordic nose. She was a rather disagreeable child other than her smooth brown skin; her duality seemed unable to merge at birth. She named her Lovely, not to give her confidence against her unappealing features but because of her intimate association to whiteness, her best shield in a polarized world.

...Success for Lovely came through circumstance. Teacher's modified grades, stayed after school to tutor the young mixed girl whose features somehow reminded them of their own childhood. Grown-up men gave Lovely's mother whatever she wanted. She took these things from black men knowing her daughter's heart would never desire anything more of them. They did it with hopes of seeing Lovely—whose body was increasingly becoming more of a woman's, even before her age reached double digits—naked. The mother promised them their destiny. Lovely was still just a child. Her age didn't bother them and when they heard of her first blood their hopes only increased. *Ten.* The years went by and these promises remained unanswered. The gifts continued to pile in. *Thirteen.* The parents of the little white and Mexican boys whose hearts were tortured by Lovely contributed to Lovely and her mother's ego. *Fifteen.* And against his parent's wishes Lovely's father sent them a small lump sum of money. Ten thousand dollars. It went into buying Lovely all the things the other kids in the neighborhood couldn't afford. Mentally, they lived in a different social stratum. Their house, though one of nearly shotgun, radiated through high opinions—Lovely was partially white. There were never any nights of hunger, no cold winters or hot summertime nights, and her want for material things were always satiated.

The moon reemerged with a pale new light...

...Before her high school graduation, Lovely's father died in an accident at work. His insurance plan paid out money to his white family. Lovely and her mother had been excluded. The men who once lived through promises were all married off. Most had forgotten about Lovely. The ones who still waited had no money left to buy gifts and the white and Mexican parents grew tired of watching their sons suffer. Their sons yearned for Lovely secretly but stayed away like the moon during the hours of the sun. Skies rolled over, faded, then disappeared into a southwestern vacuum.

*

...Mr. Hall looked at Lovely for a while, trying to discern the mistake he'd made.

"You lied on your application. We don't hire applicants who falsify information."

Lovely's birth certificate said she was white because her father was white. Her skin was a visual brown like her mother. She could not pass physically where she already passed mentally. She had been raised to believe in her whiteness. Her mother hid dual heritage racism from her, led her to believe the world wouldn't see her as an *other*. Taught her the privilege that came with being white. She told Lovely that her father loved her but in order to take care of them he had to work out of state. Lovely believed this; she saw no other reality, even after his death and disregarding of them in his insurance policy. Mr. Hall attempted to shake her hand. Lovely stood up, her fists balled by her side. She looked through the blinds where the sun shone and then back to Mr. Hall. She knew what he saw when he looked at her.

"Nigger is ignorance, not race. You are the nigger," she said, not necessarily out of anger.

Mr. Hall said nothing, only watched with his mouth open, glasses aslant with the out-of-date box haircut and receding hairline as the brown girl trying to pass for white walked out of his office.

*

She tried to hide her pregnancy from her mother. Her belly began to show too soon. Nine weeks. The mother was happy when she saw that first baby bulge. It would be a new beginning. Maybe this time they could move out of the shotgun house. She hated looking at the black boys walking up and down the Sixth Street hill with no purpose. The white grandparents would not turn their backs this time, whoever they were. The baby did not come out yellow. The mother did like Lovely's grandparents had done years earlier. She sighed while the hot Duggan sun welcomed their new arrival. The old hospital on Avenue G. Lovely wasn't very pretty but there was a hint of exquisiteness about her. The mother meant for her daughter to marry well. She now lives with the only black boy who could tolerate her arrogance. Her mother grieves. Her daughter is trapped in Duggan with her innocent baby. There will be more.

Flora

old beauty a fossil of youthfulness…
children flowing out of karma
…the night searching for a dried sun
…where most beauty begins to dissipate…

The children never seemed to stop coming. There were now seven of them and she still hadn't reached thirty. Flora's twenty-ninth birthday brought twins. They were little bundles of unhappiness. She was a charming little Mexican girl who lived in the bottoms of Duggan in the part called Usma Quarters that only a few older people could tell the history of before they passed. They were all dying out, the older people, the history, the blackness. No other Mexican lived there at the time: quarter, half, or full. The neighborhood flourished on untainted racial pride. Flora had a black grandfather who lived in Pals, making her at least partially acceptable. The migration to the back of Duggan occurred after Sheriff McDavis sent his thugs from Montgomery and Cut 'n Shoot in hooded white masks to intimidate and destroy Flora's grandfather's house, looking for the grandson whom they accused of having slept with the sheriff's granddaughter. They called it rape; it was consensual, sought more by the sheriff's granddaughter than the accused. The grandson left town in the middle of the night. Fear of returning to Pals made the grandfather stay in Duggan. Flora grew up on Thirteenth Street in a small blue and white house. The windows were dirty and the front door jammed shut. To enter one had to climb through one of the windows where fans were kept in the hot summertime. She started when she was only eleven, mimicking what she saw her mother doing in the dark. Boys used to sneak into her room when her mother was at work. They played Simon Says. Her clothes fell to the floor from instruction.

Flora, as pretty as a summer honeysuckle growing along rusted fences. Her beauty came from her connection with Duggan; the full Mexican girls at school hated her. They teased her over her inborn magnetism. Said the only reason black boys liked her over them is because she was easy. Flora was easy, but the black boys didn't like her just for that. They liked her because they saw her as one of them. She smiled and thanked them when they told her she was black. She had believed in her other heritage prior to that. She had a trickle of black blood flowing through her veins. Beautiful Flora who excelled in many of the sports that boys play. She could run as fast as most boys. The wind followed closely behind her mesmeric body…The school year came to a close.

She got into an argument with a big Mexican girl named Margarita Montez who alleged Flora thought she was better than other Mexicans. A portion of her beauty died from the scar that Margarita left under her left eye that stopped right above her top lip. Flora, though ethnically different, felt secure in Duggan. Her skin mimicked whiteness but her will made her black. Each child she had come out a little darker, a little more beautiful than the previous. But once the children started coming the games slowly diminished. Boys didn't want to become fathers, especially to other peoples' kids. Not even to their own kids.

There were now only two boys left. They too felt indifferent after the stabbing. Their hunger for what used to be kept them interested for a while. Another summer passed. There were no more boys left to climb through the bedroom window. These boys never became men. Her eyes grew weary. Flora, a honeysuckle in the summer lost in the shed. She kept her legs grounded.

She worked at Othello's about a half block from where she lived, right on the corner of Twelfth Street and Avenue F. Othello was against hiring her at first because of the scar and he didn't like hiring nonblacks. He had come from an era where most black people looked after less fortunate blacks if they could. He didn't understand this new generation who get mass communication jobs or play professional ball and forget about the struggling community. He sighed as those times were dying out. She had enough black in her and her features were black enough that he hired her out of pity. Flora did odd jobs around the little juke joint. She mopped, decorated for parties, worked weekends taking beer and hard liquor orders, flirted for tips, flirted to keep the customers spending, cooked hamburgers on Wednesdays for the dice games being played in the back, and kept old man Othello company during the days when business was slow. The job stood convenient for Flora because of her children and inability to pay for babysitting. But her depression, which started when her window stayed closed, grew. She lacked male companionship. Drunken men followed her home on weekends. No man stayed after they sobered up. Regret and disgust along with the smell of drunk love the next morning made them vomit. Flora began showing up to work late, drinking the beer that was meant for sell, and giving back too much change to the customers. Financial losses were getting too costly for business. Othello had to let her go.

*

A worn path led to Blue Lake. The wind wisped across the top of the water. Flora stood on the bank, muddy water soaking her flip flops. That lake could be beautiful in the gloaming. Clear water reflected her scar. The fish scattered from her reflection. She would often take her kids there for baths. This time she did not want to disturb the windless ripples.

*

There was a creek in the back of Flora's house. When she was young she would go back there with the boys who were too afraid to climb through the window and play Tarzan and Jane when her mother stayed home and the window stayed shut. A vine fell from the sky, thick and long and powerful, that they used to swing back and forth on before falling into the water. Creek water made Flora's tender body visual underneath her clothes. Flora's mother failed to see what this game led to until the bleeding stopped.

old beauty a fossil of youthfulness...
children flowing out of karma
...the night searching for a dried sun
...where most beauty begins to dissipate

Back there, away from the window, silence and loudness shared in the quietness of the universe.

She remained heavy hearted. She limped to the edge and held onto the vine, looking across the branch. Beautifully set, drifting towards the gloaming. Her children were watching her intently. Light diminishing. Horizon collapsing. Colors splashing together until they were discolored. The blue sky fell behind clouds. There was no subsequent moon. The sun had stopped shining hours ago. The creek growled. She couldn't stop it. Her eyes kept falling. Shut tight until they were grounded. And when she opened them again the window evaporated. She waited next to the creek for the rain to fall. She is not to blame. There were too many of them.

Johnny Greene

Temptation of a woman's flesh always caught his eye. Smooth, curvaceous black flesh, flawless female body. He lusted after it all, beautiful, ugly, ordinary, pretty, exotic, big, slim, yellow, red, brown, dark. Young black girls that were rosebushes in the wintertime.

A misunderstood Booker Washington would have been proud of young Johnny. He threw away formal education before he turned twelve to work with his hands. Both his parents, third generation cousins, had struggled to earn a living for their son. They worked side by side in the warehouse at the Conroe Chronicle under a menacing supervisor named Dale. He was a tall, hairy old white man who smoked Marlboro cigarettes. His teeth were brownish-yellow from tobacco. They received less than minimum wage for their work. They didn't seek employment elsewhere; they knew if they quit this particular job at this particular time the city would make examples out of them. Dale fed off their entrapment. He made their life hell. Worked them long hours from morning till late afternoon. Sometimes making them come in on their off days. They had only three fifteen minute breaks. This was so that Dale could discuss paper routes and they could have lunch. He called the wife into his office for twenty minutes, three times a week, blinds shut. The stories that the older people tell of hanky panky in the warehouse at night went unprinted by the company they worked for. The father continued to bundle newspapers, humming quietly to himself:

Beautiful brother of mine/
whatever may be your birth sign/
We are not of the same seed/
although we are both the same breed/
Together we're truly black power/
learning to trust by the hour/

Loving our women now more/
respecting what black is now more...

He never quite understood that last line by Curtis Mayfield but that's what it sounded like he said. Time ticked away.

They fired Dale but not for what he did in the office; he died a few years after. Lung cancer. His graveyard is lost.

Johnny still belonged to his father. No composition from Dale. He started running the streets and hanging out with older cats, learning to work with his hands. While they sold drugs Johnny worked on the cars they bought. Carpentry work, plumbing, landscaping, Johnny Greene's innate skills amazed the people he worked for throughout Duggan. Calluses on his hands withered away the softness, fingers coated with abstract leather. He began building on his house in the spring after his parents passed away.

No one uttered a single word when a seventeen year old Johnny made it with fourteen year old Peggy. They pegged them as two hormone-driven teens who were ignorant to the contraceptives that had evil implications anyhow. No harm was done. And though Peggy could still be considered minor to Johnny, their age difference made no headlines. Peggy's little body wasn't strong enough to handle the growth of another child. She died during birth and Johnny, who already lived in his own house, took their child and raised it. The people forgot about both of them pretty soon. Then there was sixteen year old Tabitha who gave Johnny two more, and fifteen year old Ambalicia, who lived behind Johnny with her ailing grandmother, who gave birth on Johnny's patio. Ambalicia went back to live with her unsuspecting grandmother. Tabitha stayed with Johnny until her youthfulness called her and she left the state to live her life while Johnny taught his firstborn how to put in her tampon. He lived with his four girls wearing the hat of both father and mother. They grew up fragmented, too afraid to say stop now. The miscarriage the child of Johnny and Peggy had nearly killed her.

*

...Johnny checked into the bedrooms of the house that he built with his own hands. The emptiness made him want to destroy this godforsaken place. Karma made him stop searching for the love of young black girls outside or inside his house. His children were not strong enough to leave. For the next twenty years Johnny worked faithfully at reasonable prices in the neighborhood doing carpentry jobs, plumbing, whatever was needed. The people in Duggan silently forgave him for what he had done to his firstborn. Even the grown-up women gravitated toward his work ethic. They saw in Johnny a man who had lost his way through temptation. Each one thought they could make Johnny love them. But something inside Johnny kept them from reaching his heart. They left one by one.

Then Johnny, saw Indy. Sweet sawdust blowing from the west. He was forty-seven, she fourteen. Her body was beyond its years. He asked her to marry him; no preacher would perform the abominate service. Indy said no; she was too young to understand marriage, but the money that Johnny gave her kept her caramel legs open. She became Peggy.

*

He lives in peace with his fifth child. She is growing every day. He plays with her and protects her. He named her after her mother. He will give her what he has left. No Conroe law will ever penalize Johnny for ruining his own kind.

Bad Life

ain't no home for a po' ol' fool
don't matter whether you's white or you's black
world don't care 'bout no po' ol' fool

whose life wastes away in a small lil' shack

Pieces

What do I have left now that you are gone? When there is nothing there to feel, no longer any happiness to consider, your face disappears. I sit in a corner and cry, numbed by these thoughts. What, then, is this life all about that death is so common a thing?; and I have no answers. I try to pinpoint your sudden departure, and my mind echoes: Why Why Why. But there is no one there to respond when I need it most. Then I am overwhelmed by grief, memories, frustration. The mother who walked away from her child. Am I dreaming? Night or day I can still see a mother walking away from her baby. Then I ball myself up in my bed and cry all over again.

*   *   *

...it had happened in the room that belonged to her deceased aunt many years before, in that room that had claimed the life of the first child, whose body had been left to settle on its own because of its bastardy, while the yawning stench—which reeked of cold and stale and of external stains matted in the floor—was important within itself, until time came when the door and windows to that room were boarded and chained. The room had been abandoned from that grand-generation to the present—the sisters and subsequent kin of the first child indulging in blotting out the existence of that part of life, which, now, remained unstoried. And though the smell eventually ventured off into the unknown wild, along with the physical body, the spirit of that first child never departed. Mary's offspring—its illegitimacy—kept the spirit alive.

Self-inflicted, years after into that godforsaken place, without any care of what had gone on in there before, Mary retired with child. Her banished existence inside of the room allowed that century-old storyline to resurface: the unnatural atmosphere, the shocking dreams, and the reawakening spirit of that first child to live within her, replacing its forgotten spirit with the spirit of the child that she bore. From there grew this lifeless, inconsistent reflection of the room, with greyish, flickering lights, reproducing images in several dreary tones: a unique variety that seemed to mute reality; a rareness that weakened the boundaries of dreams, with its limiting hands, stifling the imagination; in the selfsame room where it happened, next to the wall, the one that had been carefully painted into a thin white sheet and then repainted over with a thick, dripping layer of red, filled with streaking lumps that vanished into the base of the wall—an empty creation of unconscious thought that held silence within the laughter—the nothingness that had become her life. Color scales that emerged as golden and striped symbols, but when she stared at it continuously she could only see this wavy impression of invisible darkness; sterile and complete; and there was this little mushy image trapped in a dark, dark existence where there is no exit. She chanted the visions of her horrors by night to her family: the blood, the crowded emptiness, the red darkness—but no one believed her because they thought she was crazy, that the eyes of delusion had placed a veil over her face so that she could not see into the day.

(Because of that, sunshine had been weakened.)

Those days were not real. Neither was the wall. Nothing but pain and hurt existed there, so Mary tore down the wall and everything that it consisted of: compound paints, a yellowish-colored wallpaper, thick, soundproof sheetrock, and rebuilt, in hopes that she could escape her dreary existence; but what she found existing beneath was not what she had expected:

Inside there was silence. Coldness and silence.

Outside there is silence—and all around everything seemed motionless, ejected, still. And outside there is but coldness. Now, silence is spaceless.

She would lay her head down and ask God to make everything right . . .

* * *

Mustard yellows, navy blues and violets blending in the night. Pea greens, blood reds and tans prancing in the sunshine. Pale tinctures here and there, along with Black and grey obscuring things, obscuring life. That is why her mind always wandered into that afterlife in the sky. Deep in the horizon, where the sky is friendly and the colors clash, there is a life for her. But when she followed that horizon it led her to a lake and the lake turned against her. And that is why her baby was found floating in a river.

* * *

There is a sun that shines to the east of the world without revelation. It glistens, though very light, through the cloud-capped base of the horizon. Orange and red, hanging low in the sky; rays beaming without heat—constant and sparkling — *in absentia* and there.

* * *

However bright were the days that followed, Mary's vision did not flourish as a result. Because the baby cried a lot and because it came amidst changing seasons, her contact with sunshine dwindled. Right before and during the baby's teething period, when the days were most brightly lit, was, for Mary, her greatest span of unhappiness. In the dining room, amongst the family but polarized at some point, she and her baby sitting at one end of the table, Mary suffered. Her tears went unseen. To them, they did not exist; but to her they were immortal, shaking her cheeks like the masterful Yemaya generating angry tides. All Mary wanted was a chance to find out what being happy was all about. But where, exactly, was happiness to be found? No place that she could think of held that answer.

Sometimes, when Mary was unhappy, she preferred to be alone. She stood on African shores waiting for hope to sail in...

* * *

Strangely, those first few years inched by bit by bit, as if trying to feel its way through an overabundance of stickweed. Solitude—the baby—grew like the years: slow, ragged, painful. She was like the wild seed that sprouted unaided in foreign deserts.

For nine years, which seemed centurial, that is how mother and daughter existed—a strange and twisted relationship: Solitude, a visiting star in the night, and Mary Tiler, the immediate darkness, the edges of light.

*

Mary found comfort in her daughter's autonomy. It gave her an unrecognizable pleasure that, even through the guilt, she could not pretend did not exist. This freedom—or separation rather—worked out well for Mary but not so for her daughter. She did not feel free. There was no sense of independence. Other than her freedom to dream she felt entrapped, as if she could not separate herself from the innards of a lonely dream. Somewhere, there is a girl who cries for attention; but in space, where there is only twinkling stars and darkness, her cries are not heard; in this same place, somewhere, unknown, she searches for binding love. It is not found. Doors are closed. Laughter is broken. Windows are jammed. And unity becomes individuality.

She was close to happiness and yet she had to travel so far to reach it.

She is afraid.

She screams out her fears.

But she is the only one who can hear herself speak.

Her entrapment was hers alone and there was nothing she could do to change it, but to go on and on in her unutterable existence, trapped, cringed, unjustified. Her immediate surroundings were discouraging if anything. There was always this reflection of sheer hopelessness. Where was her happy life? Why couldn't she live her life as an entire element, instead of existing always, only in singularity?

She had not sought freedom and found that the attention she desired did not breathe.

* * *

At one point darkness was static. Nights came but never went. They were long, bleak, and wintry nights that lingered on and on. So when the sun rose and the blue sky appeared neither mother nor daughter could distinguish between light and dark.

And it wasn't as if this lack of light brought any closeness between them because for Solitude it was an unrefined key into infinite darkness where things of permanence perished without losing existence. She was alive but dead, and Mary was killing off this hybrid existence. Once Mary killed all the death it was impossible for her to die.

Solitude found solace in the basement.

She was alone but happy. But down there, in that icy basement, she felt strange. Her eyes were always burning, as if she had something in them; and her skin burnt but inside she was not warm.

*

Slow and painstaking days. Moving as if ailed by a white disease. Careless. Wonder-less. That is how they passed; that is how young Solitude took sick; that is how her mind became delusional; that is how she saw things in front of her that no one else could see; things that had faces very similar to hers; things that changed form and confused her. These things had human voices and they talked back to her, not just when she was alone or in her dreams but also when she was surrounded by other humans. It wasn't long before she started responding to these voices and screaming at them to leave her alone; family alienation followed. Then came the never-ending visions of patricide without a clear image of her biological father; and in her mind lived another image: she could see a man, not very tall, standing above her, laughing and calling her a bastard baby and she could not touch it like there was really nothing there for her to touch and it moved back every time she reached out her hand. Then the image became distorted; then it became amorphous to her very sight; and slowly it faded away until all matter was unseen.

* * *

She washed her hands over and over until they were raw and blood was pouring into the sink, thinking that that blood was from her baby . . .

* * *

Mary saw a lot of things in Black and white, not because those were their natural colors but because the more and more she tried to resist reality—things as they were—the more they faded like a picture that exists only in the mind and is pulled further and further away from the mental eye.

*

Thus, she opted to let her child suffer, as she had suffered, in lonesomeness and in pain; and since she had been stripped of the darkest tiles that found her youth, she secretly prayed the same would become true of her daughter; cutting the lines that bound light to day; sheltering her within an inescapable room jam-packed with memories; to take away her child-like vanity; detaching the physical self from that part that was pride; then leave her alone and bruised in the basement under the same stairs where she had found comfort. It would be like taking broken beauty and mending it into the no-longer-existing.

*

She could feel, unreal as it was, a huge wet spot, which, from its taste, seemed to be blood; and she could still hear and see both the gun shot ringing in her ears and the spark.

*

Three years. Measured and linear. Flowing as if trying to defeat the currents of a river. The dead husband; the ethereal lover; Misses Tiler. A flower that opened itself up for suckling. The summer; the sunshine; things of happiness; things of beauty. Unlike anything ever imagined. That fades into the oppressive night, and comes out as love. Without the uniqueness. As a desire. Devoid of craving. A slow mechanization which leads to a broken process: the droning sound of squeaking cogs; time after time; again and again; year after year; and what remained is a move from within, a standing on the inside looking out.

Mary's voice had been severed. She, with the push of a button, was forever muted, except for the occasional moans of pleasure.

Suspended, uninteresting, unmoving years.

They brought Mary shame, unpackaged, as if to show her a fourth dimension of sorrow. She did it maybe because of her need to feel wanted. But after she became big with child the husband began to avoid contact with her, just as her lover had when his needs were sufficed. They were now ghosts; unexacting ghosts who Mary was unsure ever existed. The spirit from the room of the first child enveloped her mind. Her reality came in pieces; truth came in pieces. She was unsure if she should fear reality, at least psychologically; her eyes held the rage that comes from nightmares. And that left her alone and sad. She kept herself locked up in her room because it was only there, in the midst of four paint-less walls and inanimate objects, that she felt wanted. She did nothing really but sit in a chair and stare. Hardly could she be found eating and her body slimmed in contrast to her swelling stomach, causing the near death of her baby; but it was not to be.

Oddly enough, with the diligence of nostalgia, it felt good to her sometimes when she thought about it after it all had ended. And constantly she found herself dreaming about it, reaching for it. Somehow it didn't seem like that bad a transgression and soon it passed over her that if she were to have a miscarriage she would possibly be able to regain that afore existent, chimerical happiness. And maybe if she started talking suicidally she could recover the attention that had once made her a household favorite. Or, maybe if she told her dead husband that the baby wasn't his but another man's, and made herself believe it too, things could go back to being the same. But things would never be the same again. All that was left were dreams: those of happiness; those of longing; but it seemed to be those nonsingular dreams which guide the unconscious mind that she strove for—longing for happiness and achieving it.

Then her dream caught up with her, and all of the things that she once considered 'okay' transitioned into the shamefulness in which they really were. 'Mystification' with her lover. She did not think of her dead husband. He was unthinkable, unthought, which allowed her to wallow in a false sense of happiness. But Mary knew that she was living in a false world each and every time she thought that she had been happy, or that she had been loved within the family, or that those 'good ole days' were to return. Impossible.

By the time she was able to amass the pieces of her dream into absolute wholeness it was too late.

Her body started to change like the ugly

duckling into the swan, but in reverse. There was no specific chronology but the plumpness seemed to materialize first, followed by the tiredness. There were bags under her eyes that seemed to have a parallel effect with the swelling and fatigue. Hunger came suddenly with the lack of appetite and the notion of herself was that she was ugly. Her ethereal lover and dead husband would never love her again!

The first thing that came to her mind was to force herself to have that miscarriage; then it left. But as varying as she was in emotion the thought unconsciously crawled back into the tree of her mind and built a nest.

*   *   *

She kept her pregnancy at fifteen and yet in some way she considered it sinful and every night on her knees she prayed to God for forgiveness because she knew that she would never be able to love this ill-gotten child. And sometimes her prayers were born out of hatred. And her daughter became pregnant at thirteen, and at fourteen she had a miscarriage. At fifteen she was placed in a sanitarium for youths—claiming that the father of her child did not exist—and at sixteen she ran away. But not to the streets like normal runaways, but to a lake, past Thirteenth Street, past the dump, right before Porter Road, somewhere in the interstices of the woods, to a sort of paradise. And what a paradise it was! Inside and out was distinguished by beauty. Knotted trees sat on the edge of this lake, which made her special place appear as a painting. And that's just what it was to her, a place real but at the same time imaginative, and for her alone. She named the lake Blue Lake because of its sparkling blue water. She went there for the peace that it provided; but it was because of the seclusion that she became attached to it. The southern winds that bent the grass playfully bent her heart and in a similar vein, the sky that was reflected by still waters gave her no remembrances of her dead, unborn baby. She was content with life.

And then all of a sudden one day the lake went bad and something came and destroyed the peace and the wind no longer blew calmly and the waters were no longer still and the days were turned into nights. It was in this lake that she tried to or thought about drowning herself. (No one knew that she had died in the bottom of that lake already and that a piece of her spirit was left somewhere down there.)

Yet and still, she grew up kind of sane, as it turned out, save for the unconsciousness and the spells of forgetfulness, the dizziness, and the recurrent dreams that involved the death of her child. Every night it was the same: Snakes dangling from a tree as she walked through a swamp polluted with severed bodies and coated by dried blood that cracked. Snakes dangling from a tree as she walked through a swamp polluted with severed bodies and coated by dried blood that cracked. And then she began to have images of this dream while awake and each time the dream would get worse and worse until her head would pulsate and her eyes became hallucinatory and reiterations of nighttime day mares kept inching their way into her life, proving to her that had her baby been born it would have been born into an accursed universe.

And that's when it happened. Snake. Tree. Swamp. Blood. This time bubbling. Severed bodies swimming together to form a whole. And each whole partook of the form of her unborn baby. And she knew it was her baby because it kept crying, "Mama, mama. Save me, save me." Her instinct told her to run. That same instinct told her to stay and rescue the child. She wanted to do both, and inside she could feel her evil, unwanted soul moving backwards while her body moved forward to rescue the unseen and place it back into her belly so that it can continue to grow until it is ready to pass into the sunshine. And the appearance of the swamp was deceptive, solid in appearance so when she went to save her baby she fell through and her body was boiled in blood.

* * *

Mary could only see fragments of the sky—which, by now, had mutated into a bald shield of tint—because her vision was slightly impeded by leafless willows.

And that's when she came to discover that the most beautiful things in life cause the most pain...

Staring up at the partial pieces of sky—as hard as it was for her eyes to focus—in that great expanse, she saw a path of fallen water—blood pus water—flowing down her legs and settling into the grass and dirt. Her lungs dilated and constricted as she breathed—*hu hu hu*—unaware of her surroundings—the eyes voluntarily rolling back into the head; —in the air, around, and near was the grating sound of rotating blades. With difficulty, she reached for something strong enough for her fingers to coil around but held onto a void, squeezing this emptiness while blood ran from the tips of her fingers. Pain predominated in her midlevel, where the agent was most firm, and the brain had difficulty acknowledging feelings other than those in that area: breathe and push: breathe and push. Still holding onto emptiness: breathe and push: breathe and push. Onto that void that she so desperately sought—still reaching but not achieving—sweat falling from the sky, down her brow, settling in the grooves of her neck, blood pus water, tingling the inner thigh—foam bubbling on the tongue— self-suppressive teeth—I don't want it!—I don't want it!; the pain or the other thing: and she remembered to breathe and push...*hu hu hu*...loud piercing noises they were—from her and from the other thing—but it was the blood pus water and the awkward timing of the *hu hu*, quick, nearly muted huffs that came out as abbreviations— ...she covered her mouth and put two fingers in her nostrils to stop herself from breathing.

So while Mary suffered mentally, physically, her body convulsed and she gave life to an unseen, wet creature with big, broody eyes, even as a newborn.

* * *

Although she saw the baby shot in the head it was in her dreams and therefore unnatural and the baby was not shot in the head nor did it drown in that lake; it died of neglect.

* * *

Mary Allison Tiler. Young and beautiful. A

product of the mind but not of love. She lived in her own world running around like a perfect crazy, swinging her arms in the air, walking barefoot through the streets—and sometimes on the edges of lakes—in absolute perplexity.

The world was behind her and when she turned around she could see a souvenir from the past. Mary Allison. Beaten by her apparition and tossed out of a window pane.

she is afraid...she screams out her fears, but she is the only one who could hear herself speak...

Stop now.

doors are closed...laugher is broken...windows are jammed...and unity becomes individuality...

...What do I have left now that you are gone...I try to pinpoint your sudden departure...Then I ball myself up in my bed and cry all over again...

Stop now.

There is a subroom within the basement located just beneath the stairs immediately to the left buried ever so slightly by the lack of sunlight. To gain access to this room you would have to be of very moderate height with a very small head to squeeze through the condensed space, and then crawl on hands and knees, contorting the body awkwardly sideways to have just enough space to remove the heavy plasterboard that separated the smaller from the larger room.

When she couldn't find comfort in her bedroom Solitude would go down there. Sometimes she would sit in the dark without any body motion other than her impulsive eye movement, staring into a void, still and silent, other than the rapid parting of the lips: Stop now. Stop now.

In the basement she was only a fragmented piece of life.

Solitude. Born in Spring 1979 in some far off woods by a mother who had fallen from grace. She was a divine mimic of her mother; every feature of her toddling body was screaming out to the world. The little sparkle in her eyes that attracted attention. The small nose. The mouth. The soft skin for cuddling. Soft as fur even when she was a baby no more.

Her mother was determined to make the worst out of her because her mother never wanted her. To her mother, Solitude had come as a result of one of her many nightmares. Thus, she would teach Solitude all that a mother could teach—how to hate herself. Correspondingly, Solitude did learn an extreme dislike for herself, throwing away her life in the process.

Then, in a dark room, deep down in the basement, her spirit would be broken by a strange spirit and she would bleed, leaving the spirit with her frozen stiff and calling Mary sick.

Yes mama you made me the monster that I am today
Look at the scar on my belly

Blood still leaks into the lake whenever she raises her shirt and reveals where her baby once lived.

My baby tries to crawl back into my stomach

But I don't want it—not any more—not any more—not any more...

And poor Solitude, she never understood that her mother could never love her but that she needed to take that hatred from Mary and turn it into love for her own daughter, her first child—dead or alive.

It had already been written.

So she sat brooding—morose under the reflection of moonlight that crept through the trees—and only one thing lingered...My mom loves me. My dad loves me.

But it was all a lie. And Solitude knew it was a lie; and because of that her trust in her mother was weakened. And that 'I'm sorry baby-I love you' cliché pushed Solitude further away from her mother. And that's why it happened.

Tree.
Swamp.
Snake.

Poor Solitude. Found dead in the summer of 1999, floating in the polluted Blue Lake.

Section Four

Spirits of Duggan:
Duggan Park:

ode to duggan park

I

Swings and monkey bars, vacillating with the
emptiness of a broken spirit—stuttering reluctantly—
the imprint of an image swaying in the wind.
Merry-go-rounds taming vacancy as it spins.
Iron horses rocking by default of air.
The grass bows to the earth when it is brushed by the
wind, becoming a rusted brown, and then it
evaporates in small areas, leaving patches of
dirt that look like a really bad haircut. Memoried
footsteps tramp this grass, hindering its growth.
Wild vines amble over the cement built for play.
The basketball court is unfilled. The net is torn.
The hard concrete softens into the liquid that it was
made of and then evaporates like fallen rain water.
Round balls are not heard bouncing up and down in a
steady, rhythmical pulse. Children's faces fade into
the sunset, like looking directly into the sun to
locate a fly ball; the sun never really rises again.
It deposits into the sea and its fire is put out. It is
dark but not night. No more games are played;
all is heard is the echo of yesterday's laughter.
Branches from the trees fall because the trees are

dead. The squirrels have let the acorns rot on
the ground. Only the shell of the nut survives;
the inside is hollow.

II
The elders say that the eye that is heavy cannot cry…

III
But what in life could there be so great
an attachment that the loss of it would last forever
and burn like wick that is protected from
extinguishment by the flicking of more fire,
to keep alive the anguish,
a pain that lasts through infinity, and that
death is not even influential
enough to escape the agony,
   the everlasting throe?

IV
What used to be laughter is now sadness;
where there once was a nature clad by fully
leafed trees and sprouting grass,
there is nakedness; where the sun shone,
ice has vanquished its rays; what used to be
speech is now silence. The
pharaohs once ruled Sudan into prosperity but
were defeated by the serene Time; the laughter
ruled the park; desolation has supplanted the laughter.

V
Dreams were made, hope was given,

and life, for the first time, had meaning.
Colors were no longer blurred and bleak entities
but shining rays of life; the rain no longer symbolized
sadness or a time for sleep,
   but the exact opposite.
The sun had never burned so bright,
not even when the earth was just begun,
nor when it dried the waters for the
   great flood after those many days.

VI

The effect of which the sun was
beaming reflected nothing melancholic and the air
carried a lovely tune of drilling.
The day was bright but this brightness worked
like a descending ladder, and at the very bottom
dwelled the lusterless hues of life;
beautiful sounds turned harsh and ragged.
They sat, those three, him and his two cousins,
on the edge of the curbless road,
watching their life being hewed.
The basketball court was taken up first by
those electric drills
that cause so much pain to the ear
because then there was no such a thing as a park
without a basketball court. Everything else came after
and all that was left was the unthinkable emptiness,
as if the park had been rerouted by a twister—
with all of its belongings flying in different
directions—
and re-rooted to a remote desert

on a remote island in a remote part of the sea, unseen.

VII
The mind went completely blank. For days there was
no feeling, no thought, no mental activity.
It could not tell the difference between a
flower in bloom and one withering away.
There was no break between days.
When the sun shone it did not matter; life was this
undried, perpetual, sodden dish rag.
It did not want the reality of the current emptiness
   to set in.
What could it do now that its dawn period was now
taken away? Life changed. The rainbow that appeared
after the rain in midsummer had no
color except for the greyness of a rain cloud.

VIII
Adulthood had just begun.

IX
They never knew that lepers
from neighboring lands could control emotions.
They appropriated the only thing that had the
facade of childhood. When The Park was
standing, life, then, was innocent, simple, the way it
should be. Then life became this pale, monotonous
thing that no child wanted to be a part of. The fun
was taken away and the smiles were made flat,
like a tire once its air is released. They claimed that

they were saving the integrity of the children when
in actuality they were destroying the inner child.
Then the grass grew as if Mother Nature
had finally awaken from her slumber, giving the
ghetto that same greenness of
the springtime that exists in other places.

Some always thought the devil was this man made
out of fire until they tore down The Park;
then, they knew exactly who the devil was.

X

Grandmothers used to say: "When it rains and
the sun is still shining, that is the devil beating
his wife," not the end of the world. When the leprotic
nation tore down The Park, it is said the devil was
mad at his wife again. The world did not end but the
devil has never ceased in beating his wife.

Baker

Black satin skin
Beauty flowing from her face
She waits against the sunlight…

Her existence is cruel from meddling…
She has the face and body of a black goddess,
Freed by impurity—her birth was
Glorious—her dark skin is her glory…
Her youth has forsaken her, turned its

Back; she grows more beautiful
With age...There is nothing in this
World her beauty couldn't bring her;
These things missed her...She is
Beyond childhood; her life gleams under
The cold morning sun...

Baker walks the streets of Duggan, the
Only satin allowed in these parts; men
Used to do anything for her; now she does
Anything to men for a small reward.
...Baker, whose black skin is like
The untouched satin of joy is enticed
By white crack. See her in The Park after
Midnight soliciting any takers—adults
As well as teens. She is a skeleton of her
Former self. The scars of beauty still remain.
They will never fade. The one's that once
Knew her before it happened show pity...She
Disappeared for years, jail maybe, beauty wasting
But flowing from her lustrous face as she
Stares at her past against the sunlight...

The Drilling Sound That Destroyed Duggan Park

a low, drilling sound penetrated his dreams,
    emerging,

like a nearing figure approaching from

a distance.

the shadow of the sound
enveloped his room,

budding from under his body like blood
from a bullet wound,

adding its very own pigmentation to the
dark of night. though morning sunshine dominated

too many colors were a part of this sound,
and even though those colors were all the same shade,

the convergence of the multitude
had a resounding effect.

once they came together
they were not like shadows

positioned on top of each other —
imperceptible and flat;

they were not like clouds
that drift in the sky — distant and silent.

the colors ascended,
like stairs,

and at the very top they were ragged and sharp,

172

but the fact that they assembled into this image
  that rose

suggested the merest and yet greatest image,
recollection and thought

of sound produced by white overlords
destroying a beautiful child's dreams —

EJ

Do you know Duggan Park?
The color of the wind that blows within?
The sound of the ghetto birds chirping?
The height of the uncut brown and green grass,
Or the laughter of the innocent child?

Do you know Duggan Park?
The people who give it life?
The inanimate park that gives the people life?
The collision of hell and paradise
To create shapeless human beings.
His name is EJ,
A man of undocumented grandeur.
Listen to his song…

I went downtown the other day,
They say Guy Williams had went away.
I knew they was wrong,
'cause the Task Force had got very strong,

So give it uuuuup…
…turn that crack a loose.

His song feeds the hood. It is a story
Retold of the horrendous, racial
injustices concerning Duggan.
The rhythm guides the night…
…And maybe
He wasn't the best father to his son;
And maybe it was wrong of him to teach these
Songs to another, the correct intonations that
His real son needed to learn…
But he was only a man and man
deserves to be given for some mistakes…

He was an activist in his own rights.
He sings the song of Duggan …

I said you're geekin' now,
Need another hit.
I said you're geekin' now,
Just can't quit.

I said you stole your mama food stamps,
Ain't got nothing to eat,
Kicked you out the house,
Now you ain't got no place to sleep.
I said you're wonderin',
Travelin',
Don't got nothin' to do.
Sent you to the hospital

They said they can't help you.

Because said you're geekin' now,
Need another hit.
I said you're geekin' now,
Just can't quit.

Washington High School

They were men while segregated, men with futures.
Better ball players than their rival Conroe High.
Duggan Park was their teacher,
Pals Park was their teacher, a long time ago.
Their destiny denied. They became misplaced
Within the Conroe High system, purposely
Forgotten so that they would turn to the streets.
The school was demoted, into a junior high,
Integrated, a long time ago, and the ones once
There found other ways to make it through life:
Some worked, some perished, some lived in memory,
some fell under drug depression, not that long ago...

Mr. MT

His solemn face was his treasure chest
of buried smiles.
The ageless wrinkles gave his life definition.
His house had no distinct smell like
Most old folks homes do.

175

It was kept dark, day and at night…

…He shared some of his recollections
With the neighborhood kids.
His voice, though low and weak from age,
Still had hints of command.
He was a nice old man. Mysterious. Age had not
Been so unkind to him as it is to others.
It was the power of melanin.
He loved the company of children.
There was nothing perverse in it.
He had no other friends in Duggan.

Whatever he did years earlier to make the
Grown-ups and his family stop
Speaking to him was forgiven by the kids.

His wife's face erasure; his kids once
Whispered; visitations as silent as the graves.
No one besides the
Neighborhood kids ever visited
His home. He offered refuge from the hot
Sun by providing a cool lounge for a while; and
Drove away summer thirst by giving away soda
For three empty soda cans.

But he passed away without having seen
Duggan Park in years. No one said
A word. The Conroe Chronicle ignored it.
The community acted as if they never knew.
No one cried. His house still stands, abandoned,

On thirteenth Street, keeping that part of
Duggan known as Usma Quarters alive...

Baby Bear

I won't let you destroy me,
Though the thought of losing you
Destroys my will inside...

His voice came from heaven,
Low, high, harsh at times,
Soft at others.
He dreamt to the nice harmony of
His own gift.

His voice is not angelic;
Angels can't even sing like that.
Soulful and funky black voice
From the earth...

Women were wooed by his song;
Some preferred not to show it;
He belonged to a group.
They were more than street performers.
They should have been more.
They were in Duggan. The
'Talented Tenth' ignored their talent.
They were jealous that the voice
He controlled entertained their women.
They lost in the long run; Duggan

Struggles for glory; the Park is gone;
It is due to those original attitudes.

He walks through the park,
Up and down the streets of Duggan,
Voice still amazing but will fading.

His hope is dying out.
Who will provide the fire to save his spirit?

The white man's crack cannot kill his voice...

I won't let you destroy me,
Though the thought of losing you
Destroys my will inside...

Turbo: silent passings

the beauty that floats inside the ghettoest tear,
routinely they come round the same time each year.
we were simply ill-fated kids in two contrasting
worlds,
two incomplete seeds growing without fear.

these worlds we strived in would purposely touch—
what destiny made is a death without a crutch.
the tears that pour fall invisibly now,
hard, concrete tears and degrees of such.

now a blanked memory, i pine for your presence,

take this hour away, but remain in the essence—
to make me happy and content with your passing—
however or whenever would be life's supreme present.

suddenly, it was, you died without room,
before the setting of sun, or the phase of the new moon.
the scant memories you left behind are all that i have
i reach for them, in the greasy atmospheric swoon.

i still see the laughter, the running, semi-happy dawns,
basketball playing and fighting kids in the
neighborhood.
smoking grass in junior high like experimental pawns,
dreaming quiet dreams until our future was
understood.

maybe that is when life came to know meaning
sound-color-pain-and the ability to of more than
dreaming;
because when hernandez pulled the trigger that night
the bullet that scuttled took more than one life.

Old Man Duggan

He is a fabled memory just like the
Neighborhood that is named in his honor...

No one ever spoke of his existence...

He was brought to life by an old white

Man who no longer lives…who stayed in a
Shack in the pathway headed towards Blue Lake.

That conversation is lost.

Willard

Duggan won't take him,
Not until his story is finished.
The land keeps him above ground,
The neighborhood will be dead once he passes…

Section Five

conroe's land

My quarrel is not with you, beautiful land; it is not
You who created racial disparities and carry out racial
Injustices; you are gentle in your existence; you did
Not name yourself after an ignorant dogmatist; you
Are not the cause of black anguish; your trees did not
Hang men from its limbs; your dirt did not dig the
Holes that bury the marginal; peace remains in you; it
Is not you who built county jails to house your infant
Inhabitants or conferred authority so others could
Control man's fate; parks you never tore down and
People you did not instruct police to beat,
or judges and lawyers to barter away black freedom
to hellish prison systems underneath white rainbows.
So who could blame you if, after
Being misused for so long you reached up to your lover
Sky and devise a drought to defy their mad recklessness
for each and every demon engaging in oppression.

Old Man Chickenhead

None of the natives ever thought of harming Mr.
Chickenhead or running him off. Not in 1979
when the streets were warming back up to the old
days; not in 1985 when the streets were boiling
over from the Clarence Brandley debacle; not in
1994 when the streets were sizzling from police

oppression; and not in the 2000s when the streets had grown content. He lived on the edge of Duggan, on Silverdale and Fourth Street with his chickens that ran freely in his front yard. Chickens as discolored as his hair and beard. He called them yard birds. The meat, he said, tasted better than store bought chicken. Mr. Chickenhead had a creepy relationship with them, almost sexual. Often, he would sleep next to them in the chicken pen. That's why the townspeople started calling him Mr. Chickenhead. He uttered racial slurs to the smallest children; they were scared of him. The small children who couldn't defend themselves. His blue, small eyes reminded them of the nightmarish eyes of killers they'd seen on television. A monster. His face Grand Wizardesque, red and ghastly. He had long stringy, hair. He stood about six feet five inches. A towering but frail white man. These kids were among the many generations of kids that his family tortured with their stares. He was the last one left. All the parents said to the children is, "You shouldn't be around crazy old man Chickenhead."

He was given a pass because he was white and a bit schizophrenic. The unspoken understanding between him and the blacks at first was that he stayed on the periphery, never penetrating the inside of Duggan. Folks still remembered what Chickenhead's family did. That story was passed down from generation to generation. A few older people who grew up anywhere between the 30's and 70's saw the malevolence of that family firsthand. To the kids it remained only a myth. Myths are sometimes as frightening as reality.

*

...Chickenhead kept some of his ancestors' Civil War gear in a back room where he kept most of his junk. His friend, Tommy Wilks, was already dead. Chickenhead asked him if he wanted to try on the gear.

"Come on, Tommy. Looks like the rain is letting' up."

His mind was stuck. In the 1980s, before the Clarence Brandley tragedy spilled over, Chickenhead pranced around town in these silly clothes, yelling out racial slurs of ownership in which the residents turned the other cheek. Chickenhead had no family, no money. The government began to offer him small pensions. Exempted him from the land tax, gave him food stamps and vouchers to pay his bills. To him, it wasn't help; it was his family's money.

The roosters crowed at the crack of dawn. Some of his racial slurs led to busted eyes in the streets by some of the youngsters. Some threw bottles through his windows. One group set his house on fire. The fire trucks showed up on time to put the fire out. Only the back porch and the chicken coop burnt. He didn't realize his house had been burnt until two days later; didn't know his chickens had run off from the blazes.

*

...His body continued to disintegrate. He was about as old as his house. The vouchers and food stamps expired. The city tore down the house. It is an empty lot full of high weeds. Chickenhead now lives in Tall Timbers, right there with the blacks that he despises so. He has three black elderly friends. They help take care of him. Their hearts aren't vindictive. They believe that is a good trait for a man to have. Chickenhead despises every one of them. They are his new family. They won't let him die.

the kidnapping

Kidnapping my physical body, to condition my brain;
Forcing me to wear the locks of metaphorical chains.
Showing me the ways of your newfound slavery
Making me cry for freedom even through my bravery.
But the tears I shed will never be possessed.
The tears I shed becomes my bulletproof vest

Feed me poison and treat me like a beast
Shackle my rights and then interrupt my peace
Soon, I will depart from the physical self
Blink to this surreality, this detention of my health.
I still control my destiny through the pain, oh well,
Because my spirit, oh my spirit, is not for sale.

D.K. Schaftner

We never saw him as kids. Couldn't identify him even if he stepped into our dreams. All we saw was the house. The quicksand-colored bricks; the respectable size; the near perfect green grass. The man himself was somewhat of a myth. Some adults claimed to know him. They talked about him as if they admired him. I believe they were happy to have a rich, white man living in the center of Duggan. He owned three whole blocks in Duggan. In one lot he had his nice, two-story brick house; I assume this is where he lived. There were about two or three other nice sized houses on the other end. The yard was always well kept. He employed cheap, immigrant Mexicans to do the yard work. In the other lot he kept his goat. This is where the bulk of his money came from presently. Some say he acquired his riches through drugs and then turned it into the sheep business; others say the sheep is just a cover-up for his drug business and that no real money was ever made from those languishing goat who suffered from mange. I don't know anyone who had questioned him about his businesses. The blacks that claimed to have seen him gave different descriptions of him, none about his business interests. Some said he was fat, others said average built. They all said he wasn't attractive. The only constant was D.K. Schaftner's whiteness. Even the prostitutes that allegedly tricked with him knew little about the man's appearance or business since they did it at night. All they gossiped about was how small and quick he was. He drew admiration from half of the neighborhood for the splendor of his house and property and contempt from the other half because it was like looking at the plantation house overseeing the rest of the underdeveloped slave quarter houses in Duggan.

On Halloweens a few of us kids whose parents allowed us used to trick-or-treat at his house. An old white lady, a ghost of a lady, always answered the door with a bucket full of candy. She seemed nice enough. We would peek on the inside of the living room hoping to see a man. The house seemed lit by only one dim lamp. Maybe he was in the back resting on Halloween because we never saw any other signs of life inside that house.

*

I hated him. It felt strange, hating a man that I've never seen, but I did. Me and my cousin used to throw rocks at his sheep out of spite. In the summers we would spray paint his side wall. Each time his underpaid, immigrant workers repainted over our graffiti we would tag his wall again, always something relating to a purported Duggan street gang: MOB, DBB for Duggan Bad Boyz, LMP for Lil' Mob Posse, Avenue G. He put his side wall up so high because it stared right into the heart of Duggan; it was his way of separation without separating. He did not have to look into the Dugganized rubbish.

Maybe there never existed a man named D.K. Schaftner. Maybe the white people made the man up; the black people were gullible enough to believe any tale white people told. The Conroe Chronicle never printed stories about his death. The people seemed amazed by this man although he never helped Duggan rise. It seems that he only used those extra two-story houses to store the rumored drugs that pile into Duggan that the county use to lock as many up as they possibly can; no one stayed in them. Because he was white, no one who claimed any of the street gangs had the courage to rob him. They robbed other blacks trying to make it; stole from their mother; broke into their aunties and cousins houses; car-jacked the poorest of the poor, but none had the audacity to take from the one house in Duggan that could afford a loss or two.

He was about as real as the crack epidemic; he was a disease and part of the Duggan problem, and he was safe until died...

Section Six

Sammie's

Every journey begins with hope. His journey was haunted by the angry spirits of Duggan: the wild, personal relationships of the people, the various black faces, the places of leisure—the juke joints—where anything could happen because they were open at any time and to anybody. He used to run from such crowds but this time loneliness caused him to surrender.

"What's happening?" came through the night of a local wino.

"Just checking out the scenery," George replied.

"Don't see you here much," came another voice. This time a woman, an old classmate.

"I don't get out too often nowadays."

"Have fun," the woman said before taking a long swig of a strawberry creamed flavored Mad Dog 20/20.

He walked in and took a look around. It was just like he imagined it would be—people dancing, people smoking, people drinking, music playing, cursing, and beautiful, beautiful black women. But only one woman mattered. Only one stood out from the rest of the partygoers. She was persuasive in her blue dress that rode up her smooth brown thighs. The music was blaring; she danced to one of his favorite songs, 'Southern Girl,' by Maze.

She hummed along, "Southern girl don't know…"

Her rhythmic motions were that of a sex goddess. Even with his disdain for these type of places and crowds, he could not control what grew in his pants. He pictured her dancing for him. She was tender and sweet. Her body warm and soft. He held her close. She smelled like an untainted spring. A delight of a woman considering where he met her. She wasn't an angel; angels, he believed, based on Lucifer and others, were evil. But she was divine. Dark and divine.

The liquor took effect on both participants. He couldn't dance that well but was intoxicated enough to make a fool of himself.

"Wanna dance?" he beckoned.

"Okay. Sure."

He took her in his arms to a slow song, Midnight Star's 'Slow Jam' by coincidence, and she took her vanquished prisoner and stared into his eyes. Her brown eyes mesmerized. It was a night of dancing that never ended. He probably should have never stopped running from these type of places, but destinies aren't to be outran.

190

"You dance wonderfully."

"Not too bad yourself mister," she replied back.

He held her body close to his.

"You're as pure as black coffee, no sugar or cream, just a natural beauty."

"Is that what you tell all of your women you meet?"

"Only the ones deserving."

"And I guess I'm deserving?"

"No one else in here is more deserving."

She slid her arms around his neck.

"Keep flirting," she giggled.

He took the bait.

"You know I admire women with sensuous skin and sensuous lips."

"Is that right?" Anna was intoxicated and blushing.

"Hell yes."

"Thank you."

"You're welcome beautiful," George said as he smiled at the lady in front of him before planting a long kiss.

Follow your destiny on a weekend at Sammie's where the black men hate other black men, the black women hate other black women, but they all have a fancy to sleep with each other. So before the occasional fist and knife fights take place, they share the spotlight with each other on weekend nights with underhanded aspirations.

*

Eleven Months Later

George rolled over on his side and stared at his new bride in the early morning, eyes squinted, with a slight hatred, of toleration and not love, eyes fixed on her stomach, disgust leaping from his dark brown eyes. He'd heard the rumors. They were everywhere, like little gnats flying and irritating his face.

"You know that ain't that man's baby," the gossipy women from Tall Timbers said.

"I heard she was with about four different men and don't know who the daddy is," twice divorced Mama Tee went around telling folks.

He'd heard them all. It seemed unreal trying to visualize his faithful wife undressing for another. He stared at that globe that rose and sank simultaneously with her breathing. That rose like the sun in a planned raid to vanquish the night and bring renewal to the dawn. That sunk like a sluggish sun against the twilight, over and over, sinking when his eyes were closed and rising when they were opened. He stared at that great mound that seemed to present an attraction of jewels and lose it all at once. What if he stuck a knife into that mound, he wondered as a ray of sunlight brushed across his face? Each time it rose it pulled with it an extremely small piece of life from his beating heart...

*

1 ½ weeks later

Those eyes, once so precious, once glistening and sweet, were beginning to become dull whenever he stared into them. He envisioned those half tipsy, beautiful and seductive eyes in the semi-dark when they first danced. His spirit flew into her eyes, became a slave of her eyes as she thrust her body into his and he didn't want to be let loose.

He took her back to Sammie's, pregnancy and all, with the possibility of running into her other lover and all, if there was one, with the hopes of making her eyes sparkle again, with the hopes of making his fears disappear.

"Face your fears and the demons will go away," his grandmother once told him.

He took his grandmother's advice.

"I'm pregnant George. I don't think I should go."

"You're not that far along. Come on, it'll be some much needed fun."

"I can't drink."

"Of course not." He would not let his lady drink while she carried his seed.

The place was semi-dark on the inside as usual

so that the grinding of men and women's bodies would be 'under the radar'; so that men's hands could fondle their partner's willing bodies, working their way down to the butt where elation took over for both participants. So that if men so chose they could let their hands wonder to other men's dancing partners without having to face the man they disrespected. The pool tables were still in the far left corner; the usual crowd of goons was gambling, cursing, smoking, and drinking; the same two kids who the crowd at Sammie's ignored as being too young were there, cue sticks in hand, awaiting their turn at the pool table, a chance to make some money and feed themselves.

A man was yelling, "Where my money at fool?" to no one in particular since he had been drinking Mad Dog.

"Shut your drunk ass up," a woman yelled back for the hell of it.

Sammie was behind the counter taking orders, occasionally roaming the floor. Women brushed up against him, teasing him, hoping to gain access to his business and ruin him like Citrus' wife had done in Pals.

"Looking good tonight Sammie," a woman named Teena said when he made another round.

"Thank you, Teena. Not lookin' too bad yourself," he replied and kept moving.

In the corner to the right of the door, the darkest corner, a woman's head rested between the legs of a man who was not the person she came in with. Her man waited for her at the counter with drinks in hand, unaware of her actions. She returned to him and smiled, kissed him on the mouth, took her drink and downed it.

"What took you so long?" he asked.

"Just talking to my girlfriend daddy," she returned.

"For twenty minutes?"

"You know how women are when they get full of that liquor. Wanna talk your head off."

Their night continued. The dancing continued. Young and Company's, 'I Like,' echoed from the speakers. The fondling accelerated. The liquor took a more powerful effect. The place grew darker from intoxication. Men's pants bulged and women's crotches wetted. Cursing intensified. More heads went between legs in the corner of love. Before Anna could fall victim George grabbed his wife by the arm and pulled her out the front door.

"Let's go, I'm catching a headache."

And she willingly left.

*

Three nights later

The rain did not want to come so it fell in a

sulking drizzle to the earth until all that dry, hard land had turned into a soft, reddish-brown mud.

George stared out the kitchen window into the falling rain. Their relationship had become public all because of Anna and the naked things that she'd done. Everyone knew what went on inside their bedroom. Nothing truly existed inside his heart, not since some mysterious visitor, surely of Sammie's, had taken their bed. George did his best to think positively and not put his wife inside a box without proof.

The drizzle had turned into a full-fledged rain and back to a drizzle and then to nothing. Anna and George walked away from that first night, which had been a beauty, united. George wondered if the rain of their relationship would ever stop pouring, if he would see that night again, if his spirit would become enslaved by those eyes again.

"Will I Lord?" he pondered. "Only you hold the answers."

Although that night at Sammie's, where perfect love attractions happen and people wear raincoats wherever they see fit, quickly ended and the silver-coated clouds around the moon had been dismissed, and just because a fading smile had been retraced on the faces of those two dancing lovers on occasion, the rain never stopped falling.

They watched television during dinner to avoid the uncomfortable setting of having to talk to each other, to have to talk about the baby. It became a tradition that neither saw as unusual.

True enough he was happy that Anna was his but that was not always enough. He did not always treat her special when he should have. He was good to her, but he could have done more. Women are hard to please. She told him she loved him every night before bed, even after she became pregnant. It made him proud once.

He slept roughly that night under the downpour of loud rain, seeing images of him and her drifting in separate directions, and it made his body convulse.

"George!" she screamed. "Wake up."

He panted.

"It's just a dream baby; nothing but a dream." Anna's voice showed concern.

She did hold him and he let her. She was still his wife.

*

Four weeks later

George began to feel strange feelings of hatred towards his wife, like he knew some deep, dark secret about her that kept them several worlds apart. Not the secret of her cheating, but something greater than that, something that made

197

a man angry at a woman more than what cheating by itself did.

Anna had become something unreal to George, something wild. He began to feel she did not love him like she said; she loved only the things he provided. She damn sure didn't respect his mind. They had nothing in common. His money came through labor and he lacked the intelligence and understanding that Anna often desired. She wasn't a gold-digger like George started to believe either. She only required that which would make her happy. They were both from Duggan, but Anna's family who lived on a dead end and owned a bar in each town in the county, never really associated with his kind unless they were seeking their business. She grew curious and went to Thirteenth Street that night where she met George, the man who thought himself above other men from Duggan and not just from his rough life growing up, but because he had always wanted to be something more than a warehouse worker, drug pusher, or someone who dreamed of playing pro ball.

*

Anna was gifted as a child, always seen as the one who would rise above the aftereffects of ghetto origins. Her parents raised her to have a certain air about herself, taught her to be better than the Duggan natives, to never trust or love what Duggan offered.

"Just look at our house. Look at our yard. Look at what your father has provided for us through hard work and schooling," the mother said to a young Anna.

"Look how well your mother dresses and the dignity in which she carries herself," the father said, instilling his values in his young daughter.

They lived in Duggan but were not of Duggan. Their business prospered from black folk money but they were better than them, at least they thought.

The families surname was originally Jackson but by the time Anna entered grade school they changed it after the discovery of their distant relation to a woman who fought her white husband's oppression after being locked in her attic. The Jackson surname seemed too black also, so they went to the courthouse and paid the necessary fees and invested in their fortune.

Like her parents, Anna loved money but she did not lust after it like they did; therefore, instead of detesting the ones her parents said were no good, she blended in with them because she was them, rich as she was.

Her parents were them also, but they were blinded, they were old fools. She wondered if they knew that no matter how hard they tried to switch her she would not adapt. Her parents degraded their own race because their greed grew roots. They sought riches, power, and the people in Duggan seemed to respect them for it.

*

Time continued to pass. I love you was heard less and less until finally it became nothing more than an evaporated drop of water. There was no way for George to preserve it, not even a bead.

He whispered, "I love you," to the winds before falling asleep because he could not whisper it to his wife.

* * *

Four months later

The autumn breeze, although welcoming, was almost unnoticeable due to the situation. It caught leaves in its drift and held them like the artist had already captured them in his drawing. Once these leaves escaped their draft they seemed lost, like new puppies trying to survive without their mother, so they fell to the ground and waited.

The baby was still so small, so beautiful. George was mesmerized, sitting on a bar stool, staring at the pieces of paper in his hands, uncertain of how they came to be there or why. He stared at its contents, ignoring the baby's cries. Why they were so easy to find? He had not sought it; he was only looking for cereal, but there it was. It seemed absurd though, that another man could be involved. He read over the letters until he could stand no more.

"How could she…?" He pounded his fist against the cabinet.

Outside, the wind continued to blow gently and beautifully.

He read them one last time…

. . . Anna,

I was fantasizing last night as I listened to the song made by the bittern raven and then I began to feel that we (you and I) were sitting in the shade of a big country tree somewhere in Africa, south of the Sahara (possibly Tanzania). Then I became completely involved in this fantasy and I could hear the birds chirping all around. I fell asleep and the fantasy turned into a beautiful dream. I was melting in your arms—a beautiful slumber. When I woke up I saw the moon through the trees and I heard the chirping of another bird…

Two months had passed since he had read that letter. The day was sunless but it did not lack light. Somewhere there was a sun doing what a sun was supposed to do. And somewhere there was his wife doing what she wasn't supposed to do. With Sammie's on his mind and beer in his hand, he read the letter she had yet to send off...

Hey Love,

I deeply appreciate this miracle that has happened to me and my falling in love with someone who gravitates, with equal magnitude, towards me. I am convinced that one is extremely lucky to be a part of this experience. I will never take your love for me lightly and my prayer is for our love to develop into eternality.

The rest of her thoughts and feelings, all of the things that James, the other man, needed to hear, went unsaid, not for the lack of importance nor because she did not want to tell him, but out of shame for George. Perhaps he should have felt good about that, that she'd cared enough to spare his feelings by not mentioning how she'd fallen out of love with him or not saying that their meeting was a one night mistake that never ended.

*

They communicated often through letters because excuses to leave the house did not always come easy.

"I'm going to the store." Or, "I have to take my mother to the doctor." They were growing weak.

George grew a little suspicious and wanted to spend time with his wife. He never mentioned his suspicions but he knew something wasn't right in his household.

*

I love you profoundly because you are you. Yes, I will take care of your heart. Be careful and safe. I am yours; I want you to recognize that...

*

Then they hadn't talked to each other for nearly three months after their last encounter at Sammie's, and that's why James wrote her again. But, of course, he never mentioned in his letter the idea of a relationship, just his longing. Never mentioned the words love that she'd thrown out so loosely in her letter, just his need for her body.

Anna reflected. After their departure from Sammie's the night El-Ray got stabbed in the neck Anna did not go straight home as she had planned and what she wrote in her diary also focused on longing, confusing George, that is until her period was late, until the mornings when she woke up sick, until every thirty minutes she felt the need to regurgitate, until her stomach swelled and she knew that it wasn't George's, while he remained unaware, even though they had not made love lately. So she kissed his chest with her sweet lips and they both went under.

It had not been like that with James. It had been different. It had been wanted. It had been desirable. It had been sought. It had been a wonderful experience. It had been a cleansing of the body, like a salt water bath. And it had been extraordinary. The experience made her feel new. She was not under the influence of liquor. She knew who and what she was dancing for. She went to Sammie's hoping to see him. She began talking to him weeks before she met George. Perhaps the semi-drunkenness led her to marry the wrong man...

Her...

After talking to you last night I fell asleep and had a very peaceful sleep. Thank you for coming into my life and for everything that you have come to mean to me.

Him...

Your hair is sweet. It smells like the prosody.

And him again..

Your body is like poetry; these ideas from God concerning your body are well thought. The beauty of poetry is the many possibility for the reader to sculpt limitless insights regarding the context of the poem, that which is your body.

He had told her, her body was like poetry. The words penetrated her soul deeply. She felt herself blushing for days on end.

"Thank you, James," she whispered. "Thank you

for bringing joy into my life. You are truly appreciated."

When they couldn't sneak to Sammie's for a late night frolic they communicated through letters; it still seemed to keep George in ignorance for the longest time. More time passed. Anna was his, James knew that. Her secret spot was his. The child was his. None of that could be denied.

The next letter from Anna's secret lover that he found was undated but from the content of the paper, had to be the first, and turned out to be the most damaging:

...Anna,

I was lying here and thinking of your face and when you grimace, how pretty it is, if it still belonged to me. Anna, tell me your fantasies, and what they consist of. Am I in them? Do you fantasize about your husband?

Anna, I can understand when you say don't call you, or that you no longer wish to see me, but not when you ignore me. Anna, do not take yourself away from my being; do not take away my daughter—our daughter—out of my life.

The day after was cool, and this is what Anna wrote in her diary.

Diary: entry one: to James Michael Allen:

You asked me the other day what my fantasies consisted of . . . Well, here is the most recent one: you and I were under

some knarred trees, similar to the ones in your photograph, and we were talking . . . probably analyzing the political state . . . whatever we were discussing we were quite involved and spirited . . . but the most beautiful part was that we were very old . . . and I still had the thrilling sensations that I experience now . . . I only ignore you out of respect for George. I do not love him as I do you; you are my fantasy as well as our child.

*

Once, the sky had become coated with this dingy grey quilt with holes in certain places and leaked small amounts of water. In these open places, the blueness still shown and the sun's rays were able to thrive in the day, giving the falling rain droplets an awesome sparkle. That was the first time during their marriage the devil beat his wife.

He felt she had ruined what was once there. Sometimes she seemed willing to rebuild what was left but she just never went through with it.

He pulled out the letter again, the last one he found from James, slowly, as if it was a delicate glass. He looked at the phrase... *do not take away my daughter—our daughter...*

Anna had not come home yet and the sky was turning from the infantile blue to the mother black—just a little ritual that it does when she quarrels with her companion—so George had plenty of time to change his attitude from rage to calm. His life, Anna's life, their social life, their child's life, and their love life were all placed in a nice little frame. He mapped it out until he came up with this: The day that Anna left school she left behind an unfinished chapter of her life. That when she left school she left behind some memories that she couldn't run from.

He thought his wife's secret lover was a classmate. He felt too confident in himself that it could be a nobody who went to Sammie's, who probably worked as stocker at a warehouse making little money compared to his business.

"Can't be," he laughed to himself.

George did know that his love for Anna had never truly been returned with the same passion. She had built a wall between them that he could not break through. He once told her, "You are so difficult to get along with and to please."

Her reply was a sharp, "And."

She had been tempted to tell him that James didn't have the same difficulties in pleasing her but envisioned a slap across her left cheek so she remained silent.

She had made him into the town's fool and he held the documents that proved his male inadequacy. He was the wrong man. He could not satisfy. She did not want to spend infinity with him as she promised, at the altar, with a smile, sincerely, opposing her parents who were strongly against the marriage. Loving him and him alone. No one else. There was no James Michael whoever to ruffle the organized structure of the love they had. Where had he come from? Why did he have to court his wife? His fortune? He stared out the window into the sky.

There is nothing a man can do to alter a woman's position on love when he is no longer the nucleus. Sunshine followed Anna but darkness trailed George. It was the first time that he had ever seen darkness in its completeness, without any way of seeing the images that dark produce, but total and absolute darkness.

He waited patiently until Anna came home, with her eyes that could sparkle through the rain. She was a delight to see walking through the front door.

If she could only understand him. If she could only read his mind, he wouldn't have to hurt her. He wanted to kiss her hand. They could get through this.

"Good evening," he said.

"Hey baby."

He stared, gawking at his wife who, infamous though she was, exemplified beauty. Her lips seemed a unique mauve in the dimly lit room and he wanted to touch them. Her eyes sparkled like they did at Sammie's, but they were evil. They had a wickedly beautiful glimmer to them when he looked into them.

"Anna, we need to talk."

His voice was calm, in fact too calm.

"What is it George? I'm tired."

"Tired from what?"

"What do you want George?"

"Never mind. Just listen baby, and let me finish before you speak." He paused.

"Okay, say what it is you have to say."

"Please Anna. It's important for me to run straight through this with no interruptions."

"The floor is yours."

"Anna, don't, say nothin', just listen."

"What are you talking about George?"

He looked deep into her eyes, the eyes that belonged to him to see where she was sorry, to see where everything would be alright.

"Could you please just sit down?" She sat down in the chair beside her. Anna felt slight fear and confusion, not knowing what was running through her husband's mind at the time. "Right here beside me," he continued.

She finally moved next to her husband. He touched her on the cheek and she smiled her smile for him. It did please him.

"Do you remember when we first started datin',

baby? How your eyes sparkled?"

She sighed, "I remember."

"I told you your eyes were sparklin'. Remember? That day in the rain. Please tell me you remember."

"I do." She sighed again. "What is this about George?"

"Your eyes, baby, what happened to them? Why don't they sparkle any longer, like they used to? When I look at them I see hatred."

"In my eyes?"

He looked into his wife's eyes again. His face was very calm as he spoke. His hand shook.

"Anna, my supposed to be queen, who is James?"

His voice had slightly raised.

He remained calm in the face, awaiting his answer, which never came. Anna bit her bottom lip and folded her arms and George walked out of the front door.

He imagined Anna loving another man, tongue kissing and sweating in the dark in the corner of Sammies.

*

You gone be mine. I don't care about your past.
Yes, honey, yes.
I don't care about your husband.
Yes, honey, yes.

We gone run away too.
Yes, honey, yes.
Start a new life, far away from this place.
Yes, honey, yes.

*

Love inside of love, that is what happens at Sammie's on weekends for the lonely.

*

Night grew darker by the hour, as if the sky was being layered by thick, black quilts. The original bodies of light were lifeless. George and Anna relaxed on their reserved sides of bed like two exiles, separated by a mythical border, divorced by their thoughts. Anna stared at the ceiling, eyes wide, seeing the red splotches that occur to the sight when one attempts to see into the dark. They were like little meaningless blobs with faces and she could see James's face and George's face and she knew then what her heart wanted.

The following morning was bright. George woke before his wife because he had not really slept. Columns of light from the first sun of the new month nudged Anna awake and when her eyes were open she saw George positioned by the window, sitting, staring, drooling.

"Why aren't you at work, honey?"

"Don't feel like goin'."

"Okay crazy. When are you going to go back?"

"Don't know."

Through the night George had decided to skip work and not talk to his wife. This way, he figured, he could make Anna suffer without resulting to violence. However, Anna had already foresaw her future but George did not know. If he did he could have saved himself the trouble of trashing his appearance, his remaining manhood, his landscaping business.

So it had been done and now whatever came would come.

Anna let her unanswered question ride and reasoned, "There isn't any use in trying to talk some sense into a person that is stuck in his ways. Do you want any breakfast?"

He grunted.

"I think I'll cook eggs and bacon today. Is that okay with you? Along with some pancakes and grits or oatmeal. Which one?"

George sucked on his teeth. The men of Sammie's flashed through his mind; the things they did; the people they slept with; the lives they ruined without concern but in celebration. They were bacon because they filled women up. He was only an egg, a weak outer shell that could not protect or satisfy a woman.

"I'll do grits because I know oatmeal makes you

nauseous," she continued.

Anna stared at the back of George's head and smiled. She smiled because while George had his back to her she was remembering her nights with James.

George's grandfather once told him that even though the womb can give a baby its flesh, the heart is created after birth. Though he and Anna both had flesh from the womb their hearts came from different places. Their flesh had come from the womb of woman but their hearts had come from the universe, handed to them at random by their actions, beliefs, and morals. Her heart led her to marry a man she did not love; his heart led him to fall in love with the idea of being loved.

George did not go back to work for several days. Just sat there each morning in that same spot staring out the window. Would have skipped eating too had Anna not taken it into consideration to serve him even though he acted like a child. What saved George from total bankruptcy is the fact that he owned his own business and his cousin took up some of the slack while he took time off to mope.

"Glad it's not me," she said and smiled at him one day. He did not smile back. "Once a man's mind is gone he ain't no good to nobody."

He did not hear her last statement and she left

him to stare.

But his mind was not gone as Anna concluded. In fact, he had more mind now than he had before.

"Get on," he hollered to an empty room, hoping Anna hadn't heard him.

He enjoyed his nights at Sammie's when he went. He wouldn't acknowledge the pleasure. No, that would be like admitting to having never risen above the Duggan environment that he tended to despise so much. The music was good, the women pretty. But he hated the lack of respect and behavior by the black men who went there.

*

"I can see it now. It's clear to me."

"What's clear to you?" Anna rolled her eyes.

"Me. You. Us."

"What about us?"

George could no longer fake happiness in this unhappy life. He could no longer pretend to enjoy his wife's presence. But he could pretend that she didn't exist.

"We were a mistake."

The nights were icy; days did not seem to exist. Silence predominated. The silence was a tree. Anna was the grass. The silence by George's harsh stares was crushing Anna, the grass beneath. She could not go on like this, nor could she continue to be a prisoner of silence in her own home. It was the root of insanity so she began to talk even when George refused.

About three more days passed; it seemed longer. Anna entered the living room George pretended sleep, or so it seemed, because he was crying and didn't want her to know. She asked him what was wrong because she saw, after he had taken his hands from his face, wiping away tears, through the dimly lit room, reddish eyes.

"What's wrong," she asked.

And he replied, "Ain't nothin'."

"You've been crying."

"It ain't nothin'."

"If you say so George."

Anna talked all that day. She talked specifically to her husbands' quietness. She talked to her child, to the television. Anything to break the deadly silence.

She would say things like, "What do you think about this weather?" or "I took a picture of the sky yesterday. It was so beautiful. Pinkish and purple. Simply amazing." or "Did you hear what the police did to that boy over on Third Street? How they jumped on him and broke his nose? Something needs to be done."

And all George did is make faces at her.

Anna was like the rain dripping on wood until the whole of the tree could be torn by hand.

Therefore, to avoid being crushed grass or rotted wood, she talked life into their failing relationship.

*

Eight days later

His friend stopped playing his hand in dominoes to tell George something important he'd just remembered.

"I knew this man who once killed his woman for lookin' at another man."

"Is that right?"

"Yea. About seven or ten years ago. Right over there behind Sammie's."

"Are you gonna play your hand?"

"I'm tryin' to tell you a story."

"I never heard about that," George said, a little aggravated.

"That's because the Conroe Chronicle didn't print it. But just because they didn't print it don't mean it ain't true."

"Where was I?" George wanted to know.

"Probably cuttin' somebody grass," his friend joked before picking his dominoes back up.

*

The man who killed his woman. Kimberley Menere was her name. Poor, sad Kimberley Menere. The man who went insane as an effect of his surroundings. The man who thought it best to kill her because she saw it as justifiable reason to raise kids that were not hers but her dead sister's, reconnecting the family, forcing the children upon him. The man who was made a fool while at work, whose bedroom was rumored to be soiled by others. Men she'd met at Sammie's. The man who couldn't live in a lie. He kept it inside for as long as he could and then one day it burst.

And this first child that looked like Anna and would soon call him daddy wasn't his child. She was fathered by another man that Anna had met one night at Sammie's...

*

...George and Anna stayed married for five more years before it happened...it wasn't because of Sammie's. Sammie's was a nice spot. She thought about James.

Exploration

I travel inside you; it's like deep space,
but more constricted. As I
Explore until I reach the end of the
universe and my spaceship bursts.

Black District

Even in celebrating the new millennium,
Duggan remained badly neglected,
A district defined by hypoderanged fiends.
The streets are slim, unsuitable for passing,
The atmosphere is thick, wretched, water brown,
The potholes spherical, all created by the constant
Renovations of city workers. The smell from new
Neighbors sickens the children. Trains of leisure
Pass by, slowing before stopping, enclosing the
Squalor they created as if it's a tourist attraction.
Across Santa Fe or the other side of Main Street,
They pose, leaving the people entrapped,
Forced to wait to tend to their business.

Nefarious railroad companies transporting the
Goods they imprison us for from ruby state to
Ruby state, or so it is whispered.
Depressed police patrol like the youth are dogs,
Speeding through the area at night with no lights.
Unintelligent, backward cowards,
Who beat, harass, and falsify documents.
Residents in Duggan shouldn't emote when
One of them dies; they don't emote when one of
The natives die. Not when Hernandez killed Turbo,
Not when they failed to search for Anne's killer.
Not when Conroe Regional Medical Center refused
black men service and they died.

The black district is filled with mulish, colonized
Black laws such as Bill, who try to
Impress his alleged superiors, who beats his
Girlfriend across from the old house on Avenue G

And gets away with it; Davey and Robertsun
should have been in that era of black oppression;
they sent Edward Morgell in first
to raid Sammie's and Othello's. These
Are the black authorities that preside over Duggan.

While these rising land taxes impede economic growth.
Commercial tax on residential land? New infrastructure
Curtails family ownership, and those who refuse to
Sellout become obscurities, similar to the sudden
Natural death of the man in the blue house.
He lived in Pals, an extension of Duggan.
Appraisal district lying about the price of abandoned
Land and the offspring of those elders who sacrificed
To own something are selling out for a dollar
That they no longer have in a year's time.

The city tears down parks then build new ones with
Several biased rules. Black park-neglected:
Outsiders come in, the park gets refurbished.
Politicians come around for an election that victimizes,
Ballots filled with hidebound racists so we are
Ambiguously disenfranchised. Hope for a better
Life is washed away with our dreams for egalitarianism,
Down into the drain molded by Montgomery
County's semi-plutocracy.

The corner stores carry stale food unsuitable for pigs.
These are the TNT's, SilverFifth's,
Budget's, Frazier Mart's, and the Pecan Tree's,
Who show no responsibility to the community
That feeds them and their children.

The natives let Cleveland Store and others crumble.

The cemetery Rosewood, located in Mellow
Quarters, a sight for tears, uncut grass, dead grass,
Yellowing and browning grass, neglected graveyards,
Missing signs, forlorn dead, lost graves, where only
We have the power to right this wrong, juxtaposed
Next to the necropolis Oakwood.
The people have inturned, idolizing national
Political members, gnawing at each other's necks,
Not recognizing class disparity. No longer is the
Community communized because of this green eye,
because of all the different drugs,
But ripped apart at the seams of reality.

Self-interest has taken over the kindred minds.
This is not the Duggan that once marched in
The streets for injustices done to Clarence Brandley.
No one marched when Turbo was shot. They only
Whispered when black bodies were beat by police.
They closed their doors and blamed the victim. This is
Not the Mellow Quarters you grew up
in that housed that notarized black college,
not the 2854 that struggled
For respect when they were just a nameless space;
Not the West Pals that you should let persist, that once
Thrived in black businesses on both sides of the tracks
But is now trickled down to one E-Z-Inn.

Tall Timbers

Do you remember Tall Timbers?
the place full of vibrant kids, and
mothers concealing their pain, where no one
knew they were poor because everyone
was happy? Some households even
got a father. Christmases are still good.
Snow fell once. No child
goes to sleep hungry. The neighbors,
gossipy and hateful, care in their own way.

Look at Tall Timbers, it is an
Extension of Duggan Park! of Sugar Hill!
The years have done its share of damage.

Those fights the youths once had were an omen
For the way the people would treat each other now.
Other families are moving in and garnering
More respect from the government and the
apartments.

Can you see the pain of Tall Timbers?

One mayor, who once served on a board
For living conditions in the Black L,
Manipulated the people's minds so when
Help came in 2011, it was about individuality
Rather than the perishing community.
An astute reader of Willie Lynch was that mayor.

Do you hear the cries coming from the
Back apartments?

The judges and district attorneys of the county
Have raped the spirit out of the buildings.
Those secrets are no longer buried.
The women's voices resound as the bounty.

But do you remember Tall Timbers?
The one from the 1980s?
Where snow used to mark the ground
and Betty Wright blasted from
the stereo, and the young generation
breakdanced to Hip Hop music in the
parking lot and sidewalks, and the kids
swung from the light poles?

But do you remember Tall Timbers?
The one in the early 90s?
Where tennis balls bounced from the walls
in games of Spread Eagle,
and the small basketball courts in the
front and back would be jumping,
And everybody sat on the green box that
probably did more harm than good?

Can you see the through the light?

The modern Tall Timbers of filth,
The modern Tall Timbers of unconsciousness...
Domestic arguments at three in the morning.
What's wrong with the young women?
Trash on the ground, bare-footed children.

Gun shots in the midnight, no one to witness.

What's wrong with the young men?
Selling everything from dreams to pipes,
Loving everything from hatred to envy.
Loving anything as long as it isn't life.

…Tall Timbers is beautiful as the sunset in her
misery.

Can you see through the darkness?

She never loved again. She
died a lonely death in Duggan, in
poverty. Try to find her grave in Rosewood…

Montayj

About the Author

Montayj is the author of *Duggan, The Women of Sugar Hill* and *Black-White Binaries of European Christianity and Colonialism in African and Diasporic Literature,* and *Street Tears.* Professor and black awareness advocate, a scholar on race relations, literature of the Diaspora, as well as current issues such as Hip Hop and its place in society. He graduated twice with a bachelor's (English major/Political Science minor) and Master's degree (English/Creative Writing) from Texas Southern University, with intentions of attending law school, and an online Distance Education certification from Prairie View A&M University. Montayj began writing as a way to highlight and give a forum to various social issues, including women's abuse, drug abuse, and police harassment/brutality.

He is currently producing two documentaries, one detailing the crack cocaine pandemic and its relation to American eugenics, and the other focusing on the intimate look of racism, due out soon. For more information visit www.joneshousepublishing.com or look him up on twitter @joneshousepub and Facebook (Novelist Montayj).

Montayj

About Jones House Publishing:

Jones House Publishing is an indie publishing company based in the United States dedicated to enhancing the products of the urban/black American literary world. Our aim is to provide a spiritual uplifting and deep satisfaction to its customers. Types of books we publish deal with the American experience. Subject matters include race relations, perils of beauty, drug addictions, relationships, and much more. JHP publishes novels, and soon short story collections, children's books, and variations of poetry collections.

So come along and ride with us on this remarkable and fantastic journey and we hope you enjoy the ride. We are the world's most dangerous publishing company.

The brand. The name. The look. *Duggan.*
Republished. www.joneshousepublishing.com

The Journey Continues...

Follow Montayj and Jones House Publishing for updates and exclusives at:

JHP website: www.joneshousepublishing.com

Facebook: https://www.facebook.com/pages/Novelist-Montage-mon-tayj/522720511086305?ref=hl

Twitter: https://twitter.com/joneshousepub
Instagram:
http://instagram.com/jones_house_publishing

LinkedIn:
https://www.linkedin.com/profile/view?id=166839328
&trk=nav_responsive_tab_profile

Pinterest: http://www.pinterest.com/montage79/

If you enjoyed *Duggan*, please post a review at Amazon, Barnes and Nobles, Smashwords, and other retailers and let your friends know about the experience.

Montayj

Made in the USA
San Bernardino, CA
07 September 2016